Praise for *Married, Living in Italy*

Urban demonstrates once again that she is a keen observer
of the human condition, a skillful wordsmith who writes
with powerful clarity, and an absorbing storyteller who
commands your attention. The people and their stories
stayed with me long after I finished the last page.
  —X.H. Collins, author of *Flowing Water, Falling Flowers*

Written with Urban's beautifully crafted sentences, these
stories are about what does matter in all of our lives—losses
of loved ones, losses of dreams . . . Urban's stories depict
how we struggle to cope with the losses that shape the rest
of our lives.
  —Karen Musser Nortman, author of the Frannie
Shoemaker Campground Mysteries

Misty Urban delivers short stories that entice the senses and
prime the reader for an exotic experience. Her imagination
roams far afield and supplies new twists to familiar settings.
. . By challenging the reader with shifting landscapes, Urban
uncovers the resilience of human nature and offers hope.
  —Mary Davidsaver, author of *Clouds Over Bishop Hill*

Praise for *The Necessaries*

. . . readers feel compelled to keep turning the page . . .
Urban draws you in to the circumstances of the characters'
lives through prose so keen and almost unbearably lovely
that it feels both mysterious and familiar.
  —Christiana Langenberg, author of *Half of What I Know*

Traversing the ordinary and the extraordinary (and everything in between), Misty Urban introduces us over and over
again to our most human desire: to find connection with
someone else. Her stories explore the tenuous threads of her
characters' relationships with humor and grit, humility and
abandon.
  —Sarah Gerkensmeyer, author of *What You Are Now
Enjoying*

Taken together, the thirteen stories in *The Necessaries* rise to the level of a worldview: our longing for loving connections, which so often seem elusive, may be satisfied in unforeseen ways if we persevere and open ourselves to the unexpected. Vividly drawn characters speak their minds and reveal their desires on these pages as their journeys lead to quiet, stunning possibilities: love in all its varieties, romance without sentiment, gratitude as a kind of happiness, a buoyant grace.

—Mary Howard, author of *Discovering the Body* and *The Girl With Wings*

Praise for *A Lesson in Manners,* winner of the Serena McDonald Kennedy Award for Fiction

Urban takes readers on an amazing journey in this exceptional collection . . .These are powerful stories told by a strong voice and written with vivid precision, leaving readers wondering what happens to the characters after their stories end.

—*Publisher's Weekly* starred review

Lovely from beginning to end. Urban leavens the heartbreak of her stories with flashes of humor, even when characters are at their lowest point. *A Lesson in Manners* is the work of a sure-handed storyteller with insight into the heart and its deepest desires.

—Rob Cline, *Cedar Rapids Gazette*

A Lesson in Manners serves up a panoramic view of the American experience—stories that vary considerably in technique and tone, yet all display the author's vibrant imagination and keen eye for emotional truth . . . *A Lesson in Manners* is an extraordinary collection that distills the lives of ordinary people—refreshing, compelling, and moving.

—Jacob Appel, author of *Who Says You're Dead?*

Married,
Living
in Italy

Also by Misty Urban

Fiction

A Lesson in Manners: Stories

The Necessaries: Stories

Scholarship

Monstrous Women in Middle English Romance

Melusine's Footprint:
Tracing the Legacy of a Medieval Myth

Anthologies

Sisters: An Anthology

DOMESTIC: An Anthology

Roswell: A Literary Collection

My Caesarean: 21 Mothers on the C-Section
Experience and After

Books by Writers on the Avenue

Winter Holidays in the City of Pearls

Climbing the Hill of Life

From River to River

Everything Old is New Again: 30 Years of WOTA

Married, Living in Italy

MISTY URBAN

Pearl City Press

Muscatine, Iowa

DEDICATION

To Doug—

root and branch

CONTENTS

ACKNOWLEDGEMENTS

"Day of the Beheaded Barbie" was first published by Write Out Publishing

"Small Burials" first appeared in *The Madison Review* 25.2

"Sudden Gone" first appeared online in *Moonsick Magazine*

"Table for Four" first appeared in *CAIRN* 39

"Someone in the House" first appeared in *Dos Passos Review* 3.1

"Gravel" first appeared in *The Manifest-Station*

"The Last Word" first appeared in *Talking River* 40

"Saving Grace" first appeared in *Asphodel* 3

"Care of the Soul" first appeared in part in *Karawane*

"A Many-Chambered Vessel" won 2d place in the Iron Pen Fiction Contest and was first published in *The Writer's Block* by the Midwest Writing Center

"Married, Living in Italy" was a finalist for the *Iron Horse Literary Review* Long Story Prize

"The Far Shore" first appeared in *Sweet Tree Review*

The Day of the Beheaded Barbie

This, Melanie realized after all, would not be the day she gave up smoking.

By late afternoon, the steps of the Danbury Public Library warmed to a temperature that could incubate baby chicks. Melanie sank onto the hot concrete with an exhaustion bone-deep. The cavern of her purse burped up old receipts, several half-packs of gum, Barbie clothes, and a permission slip she had forgotten to sign. Another failure.

The stairs didn't fit the rest of the building, stolen as they were from a French chateau, a wide, grand expanse of shallow steps with risers engraved with foliage and birds, topped by the stone lions on their enormous plinths. One could almost hear the echoing heels of a powdered count or a glittering marquise in her curtained skirts sweeping to her next salon. Now they were home to the after-school kids with their skateboards and piercings and asymmetrical hairstyles, or the homeless sipping the library's free coffee before they got rolled by a cop coming out of the station on Main.

Melanie liked this note of incongruous grandeur tucked into the plain and functional exterior of downtown Danbury, a wild flight of imagination beneath the geese honking along the river, the steady drums of the machines at the paper mill churning out their massive rolls.

She found her cigarette and a mismatched set of Janey's socks, and sighed.

"Need a light?" One appeared over her shoulder, fluorescent green, the kind sold for 99 cents at the gas station.

"Thanks." Melanie leaned into the flame. She'd made a deal with Janey: one a day. Each morning Janey watched her put one cigarette into her purse as a covenant, a ritual. A sign that Melanie, at least, would keep her promises.

Her enabler was John from Periodicals. "Aren't clove cigarettes supposed to be worse for you than regular?"

"Maybe. I don't care. I don't have one to share." She hadn't smoked at lunch because Robin might see her and know she'd never quit.

Why should she care what Robin Marks thought, after all this time?

"I don't smoke," John said.

"Yet you carry a lighter."

He grinned. "To pick up women."

He sat down next to her and she snagged the strap of her heavy purse to pull the mass between them. John was perfectly inoffensive, his trouser cuffs frayed, brown shoes bare of polish. She didn't want to talk to anyone. She sucked on her cigarette, waiting for the hot burn to climb her nose to her brain. Short out all the darting thoughts for just one minute.

"So," he said, "this is awkward—"

"Yeah," Melanie said.

"—but I heard you tell Annie in Records that you need a babysitter for tonight."

He wore glasses with thin gold rims and had a small nose, a small mouth with nicely shaped lips and even teeth. She was staring.

"You want to spend your evening with a seven-year-old?" she asked.

The tips of his ears turned red. "My evenings are free of late."

That's right. There had been that girl, as thin and small and blonde as he was, wisping about the magazine stacks between his lunch and break. Melanie hadn't seen her lately. She was the kind of girl who made Melanie feel too tall, too loud. Too dark in the world of the alabaster skinned.

"That would be great," she said. "That would be terrific, actually. Janey loves you." And Robin was not coming to the house. Not with the way Janey had been lately. Not with—her.

They watched cars crawl past the Taco Johns drive thru. They watched a minivan unload a soccer team onto the sidewalk, the kids bright in their shin guards and uniforms. Instead of the library they headed for the Dairy Queen, yelling and crowding one another with the casual arrogance of the very young.

"Janey's been going to this church camp," Melanie said. "It's some evangelical sect. She'll probably try to teach you some songs, then convert you."

He laughed, and Melanie startled. She hadn't heard anyone laugh all day. "You don't sound like you approve."

"My father was a Copt. My mother was a lapsed Methodist. I don't think they ever took Sandy and me to church except for candlelight service at Christmas. Then all of a sudden, while I'm trying to sign her up for soccer and swim lessons, Janey decides she wants to go to church camp. I don't even know where she got the idea."

Melanie had the sense, when she came home to their little house to find Janey singing a scrap of songs she didn't know, making some craft project in her room, playing an instrument one of the camp counselors let her borrow, that her niece was learning things Melanie had no way to relate to. She wanted to peek into Janey's room the way she used to peek into Sandy's room, trying to understand what went on in that other world, that alien realm in which unimaginable things transpired.

"Does Janey know about your date tonight?"

"It's not a date. An old—friend." *Crush* wasn't the right word. *Pal* was too casual. *Flame* was correct, but too revealing.

"I saw some guy standing at the reference desk for a while."

"We went to high school together. I haven't seen him in—years." And so of course he would turn up, today of all days, like the clichéd bad penny, like judgment that had been waiting all this time. An inferno ready to burn her down to nothing, to leave only cinders. Again.

"Is that him at the DQ window?" John observed.

"Of course it is," Melanie said, dragging on the last of her cigarette. "Because that's the way this day is going."

Catalina was with him. Probably always would be, now. Robin waved and headed for the steps. She hadn't been lying to John. He was an old friend. The kind of friend one said anything and everything to in the dark, lost reaches of the nights they lay awake talking till dawn. She'd tried to explain to Sandy how it worked: he'd leave, he'd come back, they'd re-enter each other's lives as if no time had elapsed, walking back through an open door, the exposed nave of a church welcoming all comers. He'd leave again and send long, revelatory letters filled with drawings and poems. He'd come through town and touch her hair and say "Mel, if I were to marry," and then he'd leave, and she'd fall down a dark well and stay there till the next time he came by to offer some air.

Sandy was practical about men, carnal, elemental. She stayed for the night, she used birth control, she told Mel about them while they painted each other's nails.

"Robert Augustus Marks," Melanie said, her throat closing as it had earlier when he'd walked up to her desk at the library, his hair long, his clothes crisp and trendy, his face so dear and obvious and achingly strange. "Here you are again." She fought to smile, to remain light-hearted. She wanted to reach out and stroke his stubbled cheeks.

He gave her a smile she recognized, a smile unique and yet familiar in the shape of it, the flat upper lip, the tilt. She felt a cramp in her stomach.

"Bad penny," he said, reading her thoughts as he always had. Was she so transparent? Was she so easy? Was that why he would never choose her? "I know I should, but I can't remember your old name. Melodia Cleopatra River Banks, or something like that, right?"

"Something like that," she said, holding a hand behind her back. "Showing Catalina the beauties of Danbury while you're back visiting the folks?"

He wasn't touching Catalina—they both carried ice cream cones—but he stood possessively close. In the library he had nodded at the small, dark, perfectly shaped girl browsing the mystery new release shelf and given her a look that plunged through Melanie's chest like a spear. He wasn't studying to become a priest. Maybe he never had been. Maybe that was what a sweet first love said to the girl who couldn't pretend to be casual and who would never leave their hometown, first because her father was dead, then because her sister had a baby, and now because there was no money and she had a child to raise.

Robin looked into the little face staring up at him with coy adoration. "She loves the Midwest. She said I described it perfectly."

Melanie tried not to stare at Catalina, at the delicate ridge of her cheekbones, the high round apples of her breasts, her ass like two watermelon seeds. If he liked dark girls he should have fallen for Melanie. Sandy had straightened and conditioned her hair but Melanie let hers frizz. Janey looked just like her aunt, mocha skin, spiraling charcoal curls, eyes the glossy red-golden brown of an acorn. Everybody took Janey for Melanie's daughter. There was little explaining to do.

"You're not seriously still smoking those," Robin said. They had smoked together all over this town, seventeen and daring, eighteen and lost, nineteen and floundering to find a purpose. Robin left to search for himself in a backpack in the Himalayas, drilling wells in Africa, motorcycling through South America. She dropped out of college when Sandy gave birth and never found her way to Melanie or anywhere else.

"Nope," Melanie said. "E-cig. Totally fake."

She leaned over to bury the stub in the pillar of sand next to a stone lion and hit her purse with her shoe. In a slow horrifying motion the enormous catch-all tipped over, and Melanie's whole life poured forth at their feet: the overstuffed wallet, the melted sticks of gum, the loose change and beads from a child's bracelet, the extra clothes and the socks and the old stained cloth diaper that was useful for mopping up spills. A naked Barbie tumbled out, head rolling across the porch while the body bumped down the steps.

Melanie leapt for the wallet. Robin bent and with one graceful swipe caught Barbie's amputated head. Catalina licked her ice cream.

"I see there's been some body mod to this one," John said, examining the plastic doll with its upthrust breasts and blanked-out genital area. Robin handed her the doll's head with its teased black hair and markered-on makeup. John was as tall as Robin, as Melanie. The three of them stood eye to eye to eye.

"Janey's birthday present," she said. "I promised to

glue her back together today." She tried to screw the head back on the body. "Do you know you cannot find an ethnic Barbie in this town? I didn't have time to drive to Minneapolis, so I brought a regular Barbie and dyed her." The head refused to reattach, as she knew it would. "It's like Janey's standardized tests. They don't have a category for mixed race. Or native, or Middle Eastern. All they have is white, black, and Hispanic."

There, she'd said Janey's name. Put her out there. She waited for Robin to respond.

Catalina made a face. "What would I be? Hispanic?"

Robin smiled down at her. "Perfect," he said, and dabbed with his finger at a smear of ice cream on her chin.

"Right," Melanie said. "Time to go. Janey will be home from camp soon."

"How is Janey?"

"Fine," Melanie lied. "We're all fine. Misses her mom, but you know."

Robin shook his head. "I cried for weeks when Sandy died."

He'd cried for weeks. He'd cried. He hadn't come to the funeral. He hadn't even sent a card. Melanie had looked for him, waited for him, sure that he would come and fold her into his arms and she could at last be held up by something greater than herself.

But there was no rescue. There was her nearly hysterical mother in one of the back rows, clutching the hand of a friend and dissolving an entire box of tissues. There was the closed casket with the picture of Sandy on top, Sandy in her airline uniform with her bright lips and her smiling, perfect face that had covered more than one in-flight magazine. There was Janey, stiff and bloodless, digging into Melanie's trousered thigh.

"So," Robin said, "we're on for tonight? I promised Catalina we'd take her to China Palace."

Their place. His and Mel's. "We're on," Melanie said through lips thick as clam shells. "Turns out I have a babysitter." She pointed an elbow at John.

John had come to the funeral. He told Melanie he was sorry. He sent flowers and, she remembered now, gave Janey a ceramic figurine, a winged angel with black hair and brown skin. He must have hunted all over for it. Had she ever thanked him? Melanie had to wish that angel sweet dreams every night, along with the Tiana doll, the stub of blanket named Frisco, and Dora the Explorer scampering around in the nightlight. She wished Robin had thought of such a gift.

"Here, give me those," John said, and took the Barbie pieces while Melanie reassembled her purse. "I'll walk you."

He had a web of smile lines around his eyes that reminded her of her grandmother's eye crinkles. Outdoors his hair no longer held that greenish tinge but was instead the milky blonde of dandelions going to seed. Nothing but keys and a billfold in his pockets, he was so mobile. No huge bag to drag around, no ward handed him by the courts, no rage, no guilt.

"I live just over the river," she said.

"I live in your neighborhood. I don't expect you to remember," he said, apologizing, as if it were his fault she didn't pay attention to him.

She waved and walked away from Robin. This time, she walked away.

"So," John said as they strolled down the hill by the Episcopalian church. "How is Janey doing? Really."

In truth, Melanie didn't know. She asked the grief

counselor that question when the door opened after each session. As though Miss Clemens, who had several years of training and saw Janey one hour a week, was more qualified to answer this question than Melanie, who saw her every day, who poured orange juice for nightmares and rolled over at four o'clock in the morning to admit Janey's cold feet under her bedspread, who double checked spelling homework and made math flashcards and took Janey to the school on weekends so she could finally get a chance on the swings.

Miss Clemens had advised Melanie to give up smoking, after she saw the poster Janey made at school. One more piece of her old someone wanted to take away. She pointed out, as if it were some great grief-veiled mystery, that Janey feared losing Melanie, too. Melanie wondered if she should tell Miss Clemens that Janey used their hour as a free art session and on her own, at home, continued to pretend that her mother was away working.

Never mind that Sandy had been gone for six months now. Melanie colluded. When she saw Janey get that vacant, terrified look, she would say, where's Mom right now? Where is she? They'd go into the dining room and look at the map Sandy hung there. Janey, her stubby fingernail scabbed with old polish, would point to various places: Mongolia. Madagascar. Thailand. Peru. All places that Melanie would have liked, at one point, to visit.

To John, she simply shrugged and looked away, following the outline of the church spire with her eyes. From certain vantage points—for instance, if the town were surrounded by hills, rather than squashed into the silty basin of an ancient glacier—Danbury would look like a fretwork of church spires. Like its twenty-five thousand citizens did nothing with their time but go to school, soccer games, church. And, now and again, the library.

She had always liked the square, firm sandstone of the Episcopalian church with its accents of dark brick. This had been Robin's second home. Their last summer together, on the long simmering nights when the world lay wide open to them, they'd sneak into this church to lie on the pews, tops of their heads touching, watching the moon slide through the stained glass. One night, giggling at their own boldness, they rang the bells, hands overlapped, bodies pressed together as the ropes pulled them up and up. Their thighs brushed and that should have meant something, the resonant bell tolling inside their linked chests, connecting them in the darkness.

"How are *you*?" John asked.

Melanie couldn't answer that. No one ever asked her that question. She felt tired often. Once a week she mailed a letter to her mother's complex in Florida with pictures of Janey, handmade cards, updates they had made to the house. Every once in a while, reading a newspaper on her break, she wept over an article about preteen bulimia, adolescent anxiety, teenage girls cutting themselves or killing themselves or having unprotected sex. When the headaches started she closed the drapes, lay on the ancient shag rug in their living room, and played albums of ocean sounds.

Once Janey came home from her after-school hour and found her like this. Melanie knew it was selfish but she kept her eyes closed. She heard Janey put down her backpack. She heard her stockinged feet scuff across the room. She felt the tiny electric shock when Janey knelt and then lay down on top of her, fitting her outstretched arms to Melanie's arms, fitting her legs along Melanie's legs. She opened her eyes to see Janey's baby nose pressed against her own, her eyes dark pools, her lashes wet and speared like starfish arms. They lay there for a long time, watching each other. Melanie looked at each sliver of pigment in the iris of Janey's eyes and thought, *I wanted my sister's life, and now I have it.*

Robin's smile. That unforgettable slant. It was so familiar because she saw it every day. Janey had the same roguish, distinctive smile as Robin Marks.

The earth tilted as she tripped on the uneven sidewalk. Her purse swung like a pendulum. She saw John reach out, dismembered Barbie in each hand, but she fell anyway, full on her bare knees, and below her flared skirt her right kneecap sliced open, a sudden hot stab that struck her almost like pleasure. She held still, hands pinned to the gravel, breathing hard.

"Are you okay?" John asked, crouching beside her.

Melanie looked at her knees and started to cry. Violently, without any warning, like a geyser bursting at full speed out of the ground, great heaving cries fell out of her. She put her hands over her eyes and pressed gravel into her cheeks. The weight of her bag gently lifted from her shoulder.

The squall passed as suddenly as it came. When she drew back her hands she saw John's gentle face, his apologetic smile as he held out her packet of tissues and a Band-aid. The golden sun of their late afternoon summer reflected off his glasses, illuminating the thing that, once seen, could never be forgotten.

She was imagining things. Robin had once been so familiar to her, the way she knew every millimeter of Janey. They were both hers and not hers. That was all.

"I know you're not supposed to go through a lady's purse," John said.

Melanie swabbed the blood with a tissue and then angled the Band-aid across the worst of the gash. She felt a rivet of pain, peeled up one side of the plaster, picked out the gravel, patted the sticker back down.

"Run now," she said, wiping her face. "I wouldn't blame you."

Again the shrug, the half-smile. "I would, but I live on this street." He held out a hand to help her stand.

"Do you have anyone to help you?" he asked. "Janey's father?" He carried her purse as she resumed walking. Melanie couldn't remember the last time anyone had helped her with anything.

"Funny you should mention him," Melanie said. "I heard from him just today."

The judge had advised her to get in touch. He should have the chance to pay child support or apply for custody. She'd hoped she wouldn't be able to find him. Sandy had said Jumoke hadn't wanted to be a father. She'd met him on a flight she picked up for a friend. He was headed to Mansoura University to interview for a research program in nephrology and Sandy had chatted with him "because, you know, Dad."

Their father had been a pediatrician, Mansoura his alma mater, Cairo his hometown. Sandy had no problem telling people that their father had been killed in Egypt on a service project for Doctors Without Borders. It kept people from assuming their dad had run off or was incarcerated for drugs.

"Do you want to share custody?" John asked.

Melanie wiped at the moisture glued to her cheeks. "Nope."

They'd spent a week hiking the Grand Canyon. Sandy brought 45 SPF sunblock and forgot birth control. She came back with calluses on her feet, scabs on her knees, an embryo growing in her womb. "A poor medical student?" she said with a laugh. "I'd have to marry him so he could get a green card. No way." She liked the idea of a tribe of women raising her daughter, of mythic single motherhood, like Demeter and Persephone. Except the mother had gone to the underworld, this time.

Melanie had not canceled her e-mail account, as she had not deleted anything of Sandy from her life, not her name on the phone bill or their joint checking account or the list of numbers magneted to the fridge, none of her voice messages or emails or texts. She hadn't seen his name in the contacts list when she sent that first numb, informative message. But he'd been in the archives, a whole series of him, each email beginning with *Marhaba, most beautiful one . . .*

Hey, gorgeous, Robin had said, propping himself against the reference desk like he was a regular who came in everyday for the *Times* and coffee. Coming home months too late, plugging her bolt hole and her last dream and her one hope for refuge with a beautiful Venezuelan. *Hey, gorgeous, long time no see*, and there she was, dropping away, like the cartoon character falling down the open manhole.

Jumoke was finished with his Ph.D. and his appointment at the medical school. He was shocked to hear Sandy had been killed. He was even more shocked to learn she had a child. He planned to return to Nigeria to practice medicine someday, but he'd been offered a postdoc at the University of Toronto. He'd love to see his daughter. He would love to be part of her life.

She was still falling.

Miss Clemens wanted to know when Melanie would finally reveal that Sandy had been driving that car. But she couldn't. How would it make Janey feel? Yes, your mother loved you, she could say, she wanted you, wholly, but she also wanted the lift, the high, the rich faithless men she picked up in first class, the open convertible, the expensive vodka martinis with a twist of lime.

"This is me," Melanie said.

She stood on the sidewalk before her tiny house and stared at the cranberry-red door. A pulse of pain throbbed in her knee. She would have to put on something pretty, something that made her look normal and pulled together. She would have to chat with Catalina. It was all sure to come up: Sandy, Janey, Robin's place in her past. She would have to say things like she wished them all the best, was glad he had found someone, glad he was happy. All things that were true, in a way.

Her secret name had been Cassiopeia. The mythical Greek queen who sacrificed her daughter to a sea monster. Not Cleopatra, who died when Antony left her, poisoning herself with love.

"Here," John said, and held out the tattooed black Barbie. She grinned her vacant grin from a head firmly attached to her stupid skinny neck.

"Janey's angel," Melanie said, taking the toy. "Again."

She guessed what he wanted with his attention, but she didn't have it in her to be kind. She'd loved too many nice men. Her father, his mahogany skin, his wild black eyebrows, the way he ran out of the house in his slippers and bathrobe to pick up a bird that flew into the window. Robin, who held her so gently so many times and whispered unheard words into her hair. Jumoke had that same wholly trusting air. She was done with kindness. But at the same time, as she watched John walk away, wearing the frayed long-sleeved shirt he wore in August, in the grubby rubbed-down plastic soles on his shoes, she wanted to reach out, just for a second, and put her hand on the fragile bones of his wrist.

Why did Janey have Robin's smile?

The door was unlocked. Janey's sandals lay on opposite sides of the narrow entryway, her backpack in the door to the half-bath. The kitchen counter was heaped with clutter, stacks of dolls with all their clothes, toys from babyhood onward. The unmined archaeology of Janey's life, teetering on the kitchen table Mel and Sandy bought from K-Mart on what turned out to be the last shopping trip they made with their mother.

"Not today," Melanie said to the mess. "I can't handle this today."

The Christian rock station boomed from the living room stereo. Janey sped out of her room and trucked down the hall carrying a stack of letters, papers, artwork. Melanie recognized them: projects Janey made for her mother, most of them post-accident, part of the therapy. Janey's cheeks bore damp streaks, and tired plum-colored bruises outlined her eyes. She'd bitten hard on her lower lip and imprinted it with lines of dried blood. She was still chubby with baby fat and her tummy poked out between her red shorts and the orange shirt emblazoned with "Give Praise! Oneida Lake Summer Youth Camp." Melanie wanted that baby fat, that little round belly, to never go away.

"Where's Mom?" Melanie asked, reaching for the handle of the fridge to keep herself steady. "Where's Mom today?"

"Mom's in heaven."

Janey dumped the pile of papers on the kitchen table and wiped her face with the back of her hand, smearing tears into her hairline. A stack of first-grade crafts wobbled and fell to the floor, which had not been mopped in a week. Melanie's sandals stuck as if weighted with stones.

Janey turned and marched down the hall, legs pumping like pistons. Melanie called after her.

"Who's been talking to you? The pastor? One of the counselors? Who's been messing with your head?"

Her feet lifted when Janey entered Sandy's room.

Janey stood in the center of the small bedroom, clutching the box that Sandy kept, the one marked *Janey's Memory Box*. Melanie knew every item in that box, from the two-year-old doodlings to the Mother's Day card Janey made in kindergarten. Traces of everything they had shared, from zoo ticket stubs to amusement park passes, the first lock of Janey's hair, their ID bracelets from the maternity ward.

"No," Melanie said, facing the girl. Both their hairdos frizzed from the humidity. They looked like mirrored Medusas, battling to subdue the other with a death stare. "No. Not this. Do you hear me?"

"You don't have things in heaven!" Janey shouted into her face. "You don't need things when you're *dead*!"

She looked at Melanie with horrified eyes, breathing in short sobs, biting her lip. The word gaped between them like the plastic barrette in Janey's thick nappy hair, popped open but still tangled there, sticking straight up.

The bed was made with the linens Sandy selected after she'd bought the house from their mother. She explained to Melanie about thread counts. She picked out coral curtains, frothy with ruffles. Melanie vacuumed this room, dusted, aired out the sheets, told herself it was their spare bedroom, though no one ever slept there. This would become Janey's room in time. Something of her mother that could shelter her even though her mother was gone.

"Look," Melanie said, holding out her hands. "Look, Janey. Honey. Look, Marisol's fixed. John fixed her for you."

Janey stared at the toy. Melanie's heart stopped.

Then the little starfish hand flung out and knocked the doll away. The body bounced on the carpet and the head slid free, smiling vacantly, stupidly from the floor.

"She's not coming *back*," Janey screamed. Her face blurred and crumpled.

"Oh, baby," Melanie said and pulled the little body to her, the box pressing into her stomach. "Oh, God." *Sandy, help me, damn you.*

As if Sandy were in the next room and would call out advice on how to deal with her daughter. Would answer a text after her flight landed and she was in the cocktail lounge of some corporate hotel, about to be between the sheets of some rich corporate man's bed. As if she hadn't chosen, half-blind and drunk, to step into that car in France, to take the wheel, to drive down the mountain road with her scarf in the wind as if she were a movie star and not a single mother raising a black baby in the whitest town in America. As if she hadn't chosen to step out of her wearying life and toss it to Melanie, all in pieces.

On the nightstand stood the picture of Janey's parents standing on the rim of the Grand Canyon. Sandy, laughing, pressing one mocha cheek to the dark satinwood skin of her lover. His arms wrapped around her, their eyes full of sunlight. Sandy must have come to him like something magical from beyond, scattering fairy dust, enchanting him into her world where things were light and the scenery was always changing and everything was free.

Of course he would want Janey. Of course he would try to take her away.

"Mr. Chris said I could burn everything," Janey sobbed. "He said that would make it all go away."

She made no attempt to cover her face as she cried. She had always done this, wept openly in front of

Melanie, unashamed. Melanie only cried with her head under her pillow, breathing back her own breath, hot and silent.

"Please," Melanie said, her voice scratching her throat. Her knee burned. "You can get rid of whatever's yours, but not what she kept. You'll want these things someday."

Slowly, with a whimper like a small animal, Janey released the box. "You, too," she said with a sniffle.

"Me what?"

"You should do it, too. The fire ritual. Mr. Chris said it's very powerful healing."

The memory box cut into her belly. "I'm pretty sure he didn't mean you should play with matches. Let's just—let's just take a minute with this, okay? If you don't want this stuff, we can box it up and put it away."

"No." Janey rubbed at her face. "Mr. Chris says fire cleans. It burns all the old stuff away. Just like Jesus."

Melanie swallowed. "I think I want to call Miss Clemens. Okay?"

"I already called her," Janey said.

"You did?" Melanie panicked. "Why?"

"She said it couldn't hurt, as long as you did it with me." Janey sucked in air.

"Honey—" Melanie started, but Janey's mouth puckered at the corners. She made a fist in the fabric of Melanie's shirt, crinkling the light yellow cotton in her hand. "Oh, Lord," Melanie said, and Janey clenched harder, herding her down the hall.

Next to Sandy's glossy pastels and girlish ruffles, Melanie's room looked stern and prim with its navy draperies and dark plaid quilt, an antique of their grandmother's. She went to her closet and ran her hand over the silk shirts, the cashmere sweaters, the linen trousers that had been Sandy's. The drawers overflowed with lacy bras, shimmering nightgowns, stockings fine as spider webs. The dressing table held the fancy lipsticks, the expensive creams, the name-brand cosmetics Sandy loved. How many times she had coveted Sandy's clothes, Sandy's nice things. And then these things had become Melanie's.

"Janey," Melanie said. "I can't. These are—they're still hers."

She hadn't thrown out a thing, not old makeup, not Sandy's dresses from prom. It would have been a rejection. She had to accept everything her sister left her, giving up her own life to make room for Sandy's, just as she always had.

"She doesn't need it if she's *gone,*" Janey wailed, that blank look coming into her eyes.

Sandy would never be gone. She saw her sister every time she looked at Janey's chin, her fingers, the set of her eyes. At Robin's mouth on her face.

Robin, she thought again, as if calling for him, and something in the back of her head opened. A cool chill ran down her spine, down her legs to her heels. How she'd been waiting for him, playing the game, where was he now—Mexico, Morocco, Madrid? And when would he return to deliver her out of reality, carry her into the dream that was perfect and safe and whole.

Janey pulled Mel toward her, tugging on her shirt. "Please."

What was she supposed to do, ask him to buy a paternity test from the Walgreens after dinner? She couldn't let Robin see Janey. He was a citizen. He was white. The court would give him custody. But Sandy and Robin always fought so rabidly. Sandy would never steal the boy Melanie loved.

The numbness buoyed her as she located the box in the back of her closet. Letters, stubs from movie tickets, CDs he had burned for her, a handful of pictures. So few traces to bear so heavy a weight.

Janey went to the refrigerator, climbed the stool, and pulled Melanie's last pack of cigarettes from the cabinet where they stored the liquor. Most of it was Sandy's. None of it had been touched since she left. Janey put the cigarettes on the box and Melanie breathed in the scent, bergamot, the scent Sandy wore, and cloves. She used to inhale the cloves from Robin's skin after they'd been smoking. The smells drilled into her memory, conjuring up all the things she would never have again.

The evening was warm and buzzed with insects. Their grass was long; she should cut it soon. Melanie laid kindling in the fire pit, hoping the neighbors wouldn't complain about the smoke. Janey made solemn trips through the sliding glass door, bringing out armloads of possessions, piling sacrifices on the patio table. Very primitive, Melanie thought, sending off the dead with their honorable tribute. Rather pagan of Mr. Chris.

The flames caught quickly. Melanie remembered, from her own summer camps, how to light a fire. Janey joined her at the pit, her eyes catching the light. They started with a fistful of construction paper projects, attempts at origami, cards, the pages with "I miss you mommy" written over and over in crayon. Melanie fed them one by one into the fire and the flames leapt and clung. The letters stiffened, arched, then crumbled into fingers of ash, releasing what they held.

The doorbell rang, and Melanie's heart lifted and dashed itself against her ribs. Finally. Finally.

"Out here!" she called.

John walked around the edge of the house, along the flower beds they had not planted that spring.

Across the fire Melanie saw the map of veins beneath his skin, the tired lines around his eyes.

"Fire marshal," he said, and then smiled. "Sorry, I'm early."

"I don't think I'm going anywhere tonight," Melanie said, heat searing her skin. Maybe he'd call. Maybe he wouldn't. He had Catalina, after all.

"Hi, John," Janey said. "We're doing the fire ritual."

"Wow," John said. "I should have brought hot dogs."

"There's some in the fridge," Janey said.

He smiled across the fire at the child, an easy smile, pure souled. He was always offering people things, open handed and undemanding. So different from Robin, who demanded tribute, or Melanie herself, who wanted exactly as much as she gave, no less.

Not Sandy. Sandy followed her own pleasure, into the cockpit, the hotel room, the rented car. She loaned things out as easily as she borrowed them. She wouldn't have thought of it as stealing. They shared everything without thought, without question; there was no such thing as betrayal, not with a part of yourself.

Janey handed her the shoebox, and Melanie wanted to beg for the cigarettes. One last thing of her old self that could survive.

She held the box over the fire. "Is there something I say?"

Janey twisted her hands. In the growing dusk the firelight cast shadows across her face, but her eyes looked bright and clear.

"You say, 'Fare thee well, gentle spirit. Be at peace.'"

Melanie was definitely going to request a conference with Mr. Chris. But they were both watching her, John curious, Janey anxious and defiant and pleading.

"Fare thee well, Robin Augustus," Melanie said and tipped the box. The air filled with cloves and bergamot. The fire hissed as the envelopes, photographs, ticket stubs fell in. His young face sprang into vivid outline and she almost reached into the fire to stop Janey's smile from melting. So must it have been for Sandy in that last moment when the car got away from her: one last flare of brilliance, and then the silent dark.

Janey came close and Melanie kissed her. The buzzing grew loud and intense, and one small planet gleamed in the indigo sky. Melanie lifted her head and stamped her foot and called out a string of nonsense syllables. Janey shouted in response, and John began to clap his hands in a rhythm. It felt right that he was there.

Melanie took her daughter's hand. She felt warm and solid. What an odd trio they made, man, woman, and child, embraced by the hazy, scented smoke. She wondered if Sandy and their father really peered at them from some great other-realm of being. She twined Janey's fingers between her own and felt the sweaty, chubby hand seal to hers as an anchor, a pact, while the fire bathed them in its forgiving light. The two of them sang at the tops of their lungs, circling the fire and stamping the ground, singing the departing spirits up to the sky, calling out to each other and to all they had lost.

Small Burials

GARY AT LEAST is up front about everything. My mother tries to trick me. She says she wants to see where I work. She tells me the group is for her, something about women with digestive disorders, and she wants me to come with her for moral support.

If I were paying attention I would have suspected something, but I don't want to hear about endoscopies and incontinent bladders in my spare time, especially from old women who rehash it as though telling a story of their latest vacation.

So I drive my mother to the hospital and steer her down the wide white halls praying that no one I know will see us. In the lounge I ignore the blunt and grief-scarred faces, stare instead at the supply cabinet, trying to guess if the bandages are on the shelf below the gloves or above. The voices buzz in a high shrill arc, like the lights, a frequency beyond bearing. One woman cries the way a baby does, a steady bleat rising in decibels. I concentrate on the bandages. At least I only cry alone.

"How long ago?" one woman asks in the tone of someone inexperienced at therapy trying to talk like a therapist. My head snaps around.

My mother shivers on the edge of her folding chair, her bottom grazing the edge, arms tucked against her side like bird poised for flight. She refuses to look at me.

The sobbing woman stutters on tears, gropes for Kleenex. I saw these exchanges over and again in the videos we watched in nursing school. The grief never varies, is never original; even raw it spills forth in the same scripted patterns. A low metallic thrill brushes like a blade over the bumps of my spine. The awareness of danger trying to make its way to my brain, like the messenger with the flag scrambling up a mountain.

"Did you carry to term?" a third woman says. "Or did it happen half-way through, like mine did?"

A loud clatter sounds behind me as I stand up.

"Excuse me. I'm so sorry." My voice careens off the scrubbed walls, booming, unnatural. My mother flinches.

"I'm in the wrong room." I flounder towards the door and am outside, crossing the parking lot, halfway to the car before she flutters up to me.

An ambulance skirls by us, lights streaming in the bright of day, the siren a loud whoop. I want to turn on her. I could say, "Digestive disorder? Hah! You think I need help? You think I'm not doing fine on my own?"

She would try the gentle tack first. "You do need help, Diana. Anyone would. You don't have to do this alone." All warm sweetness, like blackberry pie.

When I ignore her, she'll turn challenging. Other women lose things and they still get out of bed and go to work and pack lunches and put in IVs and why should you be any different? I know those words are there, shrinking behind the conciliation. So is the anger. Think of Gary, she wants to say. Think of what he's lost. Words floating like life rafts on a restless tide, no one inside them. Is she going to try to tell me that I've only lost one person, and he's lost two?

The righteousness of the bereaved: I can pretend my own wound grants me amnesty. I clamp my mouth shut, march to the car, wait there in the concentrated metal heat. She pauses outside the door, swaying between the fear of hurting me and the fear of remaining silent, then reaches a small curved hand for the door handle. I drive over a curb without seeing it and we both grit our teeth and jounce from the shock. Neither of us dares say a word. Silence stretches between us like blades of knives, glinting with the accusations we are both too well-bred to speak, I because she taught me and she because she was never allowed to ask for anything in her life.

THE THING IS, I do think of Gary. I do wonder what he's feeling. I wonder it every time he comes home from the office in his suit and tie to find me with a frozen dinner or a pizza thawing on the stove, sitting in the living room with the lights off and my yoga pants on. I think of him every time I pull out the debit card in the liquor store, every time I reach for the sleeping pills, every time I remember my medical leave will expire soon.

Loud magazines on the checkout shelves boast summer prints and pedicures as the way to beat your blues. Women who have overcome harrowing adversity beam from glossy pages. Self-help literature floods our mailbox, trees dying daily in the hope of saving my soul. Gary would love a support group, he's just the type for it, but nobody offers a group for the husbands, the fathers-not-to-be.

Is it fair? Gary never complains. When I wake up screaming from dreams of the unwanted children I read about in the newspaper (babies left in cars, garbage cans, flushed down toilets for the love of God) Gary turns on the light and puts on meditative chants and makes me tea. He doesn't drink tea.

He promised me he wouldn't tell my mother about the night he found me in the kitchen with the bread knife, eyes blank with sleep. I told him our daughter was trying to come out and no one would help me. I had been looking for a pan to boil water and clean the knife, intending, one can only suppose of the wild dreaming mind, to open my belly and release the child I thought was there. Gary, with his tender hands, took the knife away, told me he would drive me to the hospital, and led me back to bed.

Gary has always been tender. I remember my dress blowing against the backs of my knees as we stood in the field where he first told me he loved me. I remember how he kissed me beneath my straw hat, the sunburn on the back of his neck after, the wildflowers he made into a bouquet.

"They're so pretty," I said. "What are they?"

"Blue ones and yellow ones," he said.

It was harder on him when they began to follow me around, these strange and silent children. They haunted me wherever we went. They knew and mocked me, watching with their wise eyes, their hands like starfish, their cheeks like little moons. In the supermarket they crept up behind me, appearing at my knees like a quiet reproach. In restaurants they watched me with round eyes and round faces, sniffing the air for the blood still leaking from me, slow and dank, a dying stream.

Once in a bookstore a baby crawled toward me and I froze to the spot, terrified it would touch me. I stood there shaking and petrified until Gary took my elbow to lead me away.

The father scooped up the infant and grinned his parental pride at us, those crazy babies, aren't they so cute? My husband watched the other man's hands close around the child and the nightmares that night were the worst ever. I dreamed I pulled the trash can from beneath the sink and found child parts nestled in the garbage, arms and bellies and bloodless legs, baby fingers curled like little pearls. Gary finally put me in the car and drove through the half-lit streets of the city, through the fast food drive thru for ice cream just as we had when we were first married, he in his boxer shorts, me in my nightgown with cool air on my legs.

He had been talking about taking a trip, getting a change of scenery, or so he told our family and friends. To our doctor he was honest: the hallucinations, the nightmares were getting worse. The doctor only smiled, skeptical, polite, saying he had done what he could. Try yoga, acupuncture, herbs.

We did not tell him about the bread knife. I think there is a thin bright line between me and the doctor, and on one side is yoga and acupuncture, and on the other is a quiet place with white walls, medications, restricted visitors, plenty of rest.

The doctor likes to bottle things up, put a label on them. He said the bleeding was normal and would stop eventually. He gave me a prescription, recommendations for a psychologist, a certain kind and clinical sympathy, all he had to spare. I watched him scribble out my ticket for forgetfulness, more pills than I ever knew existed, and when he handed the slip to me and our fingers brushed he quickly pulled his hand away.

He didn't know me, thank God. He had never felt his own blood a dark river between his thighs, had never felt memory in his belly, heavy as a stone. My obstetrician stuck mainly to the fifth floor, going about her work, delivering babies, feeling the swollen stomachs of expectant mothers. Mine was the second floor, the pediatric ward. If I went back to work—when I went back to work—there was always the chance I might pass her in the hall.

THE FIRST TIME he plays the game again, I don't know what he is doing. It's been so long. I am sitting at the

Chinese place where I promised to meet him for lunch. The door chimes as he comes in, a tall man, a bold man with dark hair and bleached teeth.

"Excuse me," he says. "Are you waiting for someone?"

I stare at him, mouth opening to demand an explanation, but he shakes his head lightly, coaxing me to play along.

"My husband," I say instead. "He's very protective. He wouldn't like strange men talking to me."

He sits down across the table, folding long limbs into a bamboo chair with a bow tied around the back. He pretends not to see the little girl who comes out of the kitchen and stands looking at me with perfect blankness, her eyes like black seeds over the curve of her cheeks. The envelope holds a printed itinerary, the travel group's logo emblazoned across each page.

"Has your husband ever asked you to run away to Europe with him?"

Another moment passes. The curled orange blossom in its tiny vase could have opened into bloom in that long silence.

"He could never get away from his business that long. He's far too busy."

"Say he made arrangements to have his partner look after things for a while. Say he cleared it with his clients. Say he wanted to take you for two months."

The background music switches from something amusing and exotic to loud Broadway hits. I pick up the glossy paper and peer inside. Gary went for the upscale package. Paris, Rome, Sicily; all the places my mother made me give up for nursing school, urging practicality over romance, a tour postponed to keep me out of debt. The seats of the ancient world—just the place to bury a ruined heart. I can see myself atop the battlements of a medieval castle, hair streaming in a wild breeze.

"What about my job? My leave is up in two weeks."

But he's made all the arrangements. I say I'm not ready. He says it's time. I say we can't afford to go. He says we can't afford not to.

IF YOU LET a child come between you and your husband you'll regret it all your life, my mother warned me when we first learned I was pregnant. I knew the baby would change things between me and Gary, that it was not a matter of finite love but limited attention. I am being punished for that now.

Little eyes, tiny nose, a body round as a cantaloupe. I feel her at night against me, lying against my breast, curled beneath my heart. I lie on my side as if my whole body could embrace her, shoulders and stomach and knees. When I wake it takes a moment for the warmth to leave, dissipating with the dream. I carry a stone in my belly, deep and low in the center. A memory hard as a fossil.

"VENICE?" MY MOTHER says over the phone. "What are you doing in Venice? It's the saddest city in the world."

Which is why I like it. A city of mourning, a city of tears. A city full of people who have no occupations, who are not waiting for their grace period to expire. We are tourists, rovers on holiday; we can launch a stone into any lake and be gone before the ripples reach us.

There are no children here, Gary said at the top of the Eiffel Tower. *Il y n'a pas les enfants ici.* He swept me into his arms and kissed me dramatically. *Tu est l'amour de ma vie*. He got that from the phrasebook.

I do not speak your language, I have learned how to say in four different tongues. *Je ne parle pas français.*

In the Louvre he pushed me past portraits of Madonna and child. Now he is learning how to romance me in Italian. *Cara mia,* he says, *mi tesora.* I make him leave the phrasebook in the hotel room when we go out. I want to be at someone's mercy.

Signora, molto bella, the waiters, restaurateurs, shopkeepers say. She's not a lady, she's my wife! Gary pretends to shout at the Italians as they drive by and honk their horns. *Bella donna,* a deadly poison. I don't say that to him.

The first time we played our game, we had known each other two months. He met me at an outdoor café that served Italian food. Instead of coming to the table, he paused before the menu display and pretended to study it while watching me. I saw him and pretended to look at my own menu. He walked down the street to a flower vendor, bought a Dutch iris, and returned. He walked among the empty tables and stood before mine.

"Excuse me."

I looked up at him from beneath the brim of my hat. I didn't know what the game was, so I waited.

"I beg your pardon, but I saw you sitting alone, though there is another place setting. Are you expecting someone?"

"I am," I said with what I imagined was a mysterious smile. I lay down my menu. Two months is an eyeblink, after all. Not even a full trimester.

"I'm waiting for a handsome stranger to bring me flowers."

He smiled and sat down, laid the iris across my salad plate. "You get me instead," he said.

I took him. No other man had cared to learn that

the Dutch iris is my favorite.

"LET'S HAVE another baby," Gary says in the dark, impassioned. The tiny bed in the tiny room of our Italian *pensione* squeaks in cadence, punctuating his words. I feel him moving inside me and the liquid warmth seeping toward my core where there is only the stone. I lie still until he falls asleep and when I slide out of bed and stand up I feel liquid running down my legs. It might be water. Or blood.

"I'm sorry," I whisper, standing there leaking, feeling the hard wooden floor beneath my bare feet. The only light in the room comes from the candle on the bedside table and it casts an uncertain light over the tangled sheets and my husband's bronze body. He lies in bed sleeping without dreams.

When I blow out the candle he disappears and I step alone into the bathroom with the clawed feet and the hot and cold faucets that turn in opposite directions. The towels are as thin and worn as tissues. I hold one between my legs until the moisture stops and when I bring it to the sink to rinse I am surprised there is no blood.

IN VENICE we go to St. Mark's so I can light a candle for my baby, as I have done in every cathedral throughout Europe. Gary isn't Catholic; he isn't anything, he says, except maybe Protestant, protesting against organizations, dependence, covenants, obedience without understanding, punishment without reprieve. He says the beauty of the Church is that for a euro you can buy a prayer and hope that if God will not grant you an audience, Mary or one of the saints will intercede on your behalf.

At the Stefansdom in Vienna he panicked when I stepped into one of the confession booths and he couldn't find me. I was waiting for a priest to come hear me, give me instructions on how to prostrate myself before God. How much tithing, how many candles, the Hail Marys it might take before He granted me what He granted the least of His creatures.

At a rathskeller in Berlin Gary joked that maybe he should see a priest, or a rabbi. In the Old Testament, barren women gave birth all the time if their husbands made the right sacrifices. Look at Sarah, wife of Abraham. Well past child-bearing age, but old Abe kills a few cows, and wham! *Bambino*!

"Do your duty," my mother said when I phoned her from the hotel. I pretended I hadn't heard either of them and ordered another pint of beer.

Outside St. Marks, in the piazza, Gary goes for a gelato and I buy nuts to feed the birds. I see pigeons so bold that they land on people's arms and shoulders, pecking the seeds right out of their hands. When I open the package a crowd of them descends on me, their claws scraping my arms, silken feathers brushing my cheek. I can see them clasping my shirt with their scaly fingers and carrying me away, over the Grand Canal, to the mosques of the East. Something touches my feet and when I look down I think I have imagined the child standing there.

My fingers go numb. She has glossy black hair and blue eyes, the child that Gary and I might have had. We stand within a world unto ourselves, encircled by a crown of birds, like the queen and the stolen child from the fairy tale.

Hilf mir? she asks in German. *Ich möchte die Vogeln füttern.* She holds up her hands, waiting for me to give her some seed. Slow moments pass while I look at her, my heart beating in tune with the beating wings. I take her hand and kneel before her and press her small clean hand to my cheek. As I lean close she looks up at me, questioning, trusting. I take her hand and pour a small stream into her upturned palm. A cloud of pigeons nuzzles into her hand, and she laughs.

She could be mine, I think. I could keep her. She had entered this entranced circle, a gift to me. I could take her tiny delicate hand and lead her away and if she cried I would say, *Sssh, mädchen, Ich bin deine Mutti.* I am your mother. I would feel her head on my shoulder as we flew home and mornings I would stand in the kitchen packing her lunch for school, never a sandwich she didn't like, always a little sweet for dessert. I would explain to my mother that this is why people steal children, simply this: because this craving drives them to madness, because it is a stopper on their pain.

Gary finds me in the piazza, swarmed with birds, their feet scratching my forearms and feathers scratching my cheek. He sees the girl and pulls me away.

"We need more seed. Get us more seed, please?" I tell him desperately. He takes me by the shoulder, fingers digging into my collarbone.

"Jesus, Diana." It is a warning. I look up and through the parting curtain of pearly grey bodies I see the couple approaching, a dark-haired man and a blue-eyed woman, calling to the little girl. As she hears her name she runs to them and follows them into the shadow of the arcade.

The sun on the square, in that moment, is unbearable, and so is the weight of his hand on my arm. As we walk home I fight the urge to throw myself into one of the canals, just to cool the flush spreading through my body. I wonder what Gary would do. If he would jump in after me, or if he would just walk away.

*

THE NEXT morning I spend in the shops while he tours one of the palazzos. I don't buy anything and end up at a fountain in some tiny square. I sit on the rim and watch the water spilling from the cherub's urn and look at the coins piled up on the bottom. No one has ever fished them out, not even daring young boys who want to buy a gelato or cigarettes. They lie glued by rust to the aging stone. There are no mothers or nannies here, as there are in the other squares, pushing strollers or pulling a wandering toddler behind them. This square is reserved for old women who sit on benches nodding in the sun. I know how they feel: too tired to do more than anything but sit in stillness, wondering how they can feel anything as simple as the sun on their faces.

What does she mean, *do my duty?* Does she mean my wifely duty, or does she want me to see a priest?

"Buon giorno, bella signora," my husband says, approaching me like a stranger at the little café where I sit fiddling with an iced coffee. "You look sad. Why should such a beautiful woman look so sad? Here in Venice, the city of angels?"

A woman across the square watches him as he sinks into the chair and smiles at me. The first time I met Gary I saw only the dark hair, a rectangular face. Then I noticed the scar along his left temple and he became interesting, a man with experiences, a past.

Here in the sun he is simply a man in Italy enjoying his vacation, a man who wants a wife and a baby and a house and investment accounts. A silence spreads out between us like ripples in the fountain. Here, since I was not in my skin, I can more easily speak the truth.

"I am suffering a great sorrow," I say.

"Sorrow should never touch the life of one such as

you. Only joy." My husband imagines that this is how Italians talk.

I look at my coffee where the ice sinks slowly into the mocha cream, shrinking and shrinking before it disappears altogether.

"Tell me what you would do if your wife had a stillbirth. If your baby was born dead."

He flinches, but stretches his hand out over the table, palm upwards. "Diana. Don't."

I put my hands on my knees. "Don't you think you would mourn that child, that you would grieve and you would give your wife time to grieve? Or would you act like a baby is a—a light bulb you can just replace?"

He does not move his hand but his entire body goes taut, like a violin string wound too tightly. Gary counts to ten before he speaks when he is angry. I do not have that gift of patience; the words, forming like a cloud behind me, were like birds lifting, a migration that cannot be stopped.

"Tell me you would understand if your wife couldn't go back to nursing. If she could not bear to set foot in that hospital every day and relive it."

"Please, Diana," he says.

He buys the grief literature; he believes in healing, he believes in calling it a biological aberration, a wound that heals, a cell malfunction. In Gary's world you get back on the horse, you try again. He does not believe in acts of God. His body is intact, smooth limbed and handsome, all his scars on the skin.

"Try to imagine it," I say. "Going to work in a room with a sick child, caring for a hurt child, when your own body . . . ." Could be toxic. Could carry a poison that became contagious, that swept forth like a natural disaster and contaminated everything it touched. I feel awed for a moment. That power.

"Of course I can imagine it," he says through gritted teeth. "You think I can't? You think I don't feel it?"

"I believe you feel it," I say, lying by instinct. I see my mother in the quiver of his outraged elbows, the way he rises to the edge of his seat. The tiny folds at the corners of his eyes fan like the bristles of sea urchins. He has never felt something die inside of him.

"There might be something wrong with me," I say. I smooth my napkin over and over with my fingers. I refuse to cry, not in this open café where tourists from every country can look at us out of the corners of their eyes.

"Then we adopt," he says. "We find a surrogate. We foster." A pulse beats in the artery in his neck. "There are other ways."

Gary is an atheist, practically pagan; he doesn't understand about Eve, the sins of the mother. He doesn't understand that I might kill any child who comes to me, from my body or otherwise, that I might carry some evil in my blood. He is as pure as the sun.

I put out a hand that stops halfway across the table. "What if I can't—?"

I can't say the word *mother*. It congeals in my mouth, like the other things inside me that have hardened, become resistant.

He looks at me with the face of a sphinx, a blank impasse, an immensity of stone that I could never hope to scale.

"I can't do this right now," he says. "I can't be here."

He stands, folds the napkin on his plate in a precise triangle, and leaves, joining the traffic on the street, winding through the narrow alleyway where windows lined with boxed flowers looked down onto the stones.

This is it, I think, one of those moments where life

cracks and a huge portion falls away, like an ice floe from a glacier. A fissure growing for years indiscernible to someone outside, while inside, those involved stepped carefully around it, neither wanting to begin the tremor that made the whole monolith dissolve. Still and numb at the café table, with my iced coffee warming, I envision Gary at our *pensione*, packing his things, paying the bill. He would prop my plane ticket up on the bureau where I would be sure to see it. I try to breathe deeply. Beside the ticket he would leave the last of his euros. He would do that much.

When I see him coming back through the crowd, I cannot say if the tightness in my stomach is relief or regret.

He sits down, pulls his napkin across his lap, opens his menu. He speaks to the server but not to me. I keep quiet when the antipasti arrives. Over the gazpacho I want to say I'm sorry, but the words sit in my chest like a balloon filled with water. By the time the pasta is served I am desperate to speak.

"These mussels—do you suppose they were caught this morning?"

"They're a little chewy," he says.

I do not want to argue. In Venice there are alleys, there are bridges that lead nowhere, that lift you up into a blank wall. Gary always laughs when I toss aside the map. Sometimes there is no need for things to connect, to be explained.

"How was the palazzo?"

"I didn't finish the tour." He looks up. "We could go back this afternoon."

Behind my sunglasses, where I know he can't see, I close my eyes. "Yes, please."

He smiles then, and his body relaxes, his big shoulders releasing, his hands unclenched. The hole I tore open will be avoided, not mentioned again.

"But," he insists, "you must only speak in Italian."

Hungry as a tourist, he finishes all the food but the mussels, leaving them on their half-shells, exposed and naked. We spend the afternoon wandering through the palace of some long-dead Italian duke, holding hands and commenting on the ancestors lined in gilt against the wall. Pigeons coo from the upper reaches of the gallery and in the cool shadowed alcoves he pulls me aside to kiss me.

On the way back to the hotel after dinner, swaying under a Venice moon, he pays the gondolier to serenade us. I listen to the liquid swish of the oars and wonder if I should just come to accept, finally, that even when I am with him there will be these moments when the distance between us is that of the earth to the stars. When I am utterly and completely alone.

HE SLEEPS SO soundly, and I am alone again in this room, with a strange moon drifting on the horizon. I feel burdened by the impossibility of words.

Our window looks out on a side canal, with a tiny footbridge and flowers growing in the box. The casement is barred but the wide windowsill has a tiled ledge and a bench wide enough to sit on. In the moonlight the distance takes on a different aspect. Hard surfaces are warmer, softer surfaces remote.

For five nights now I have sat here, running my hands over the cool tile, feeling on my face the cool moon. I like to wonder about the people who have lived in this city. The men, the lovers, who were sent away to fight in the duke's army; the young girls, pregnant with shame, who threw themselves into the canal. If I die here, in Venice, I want my soul to haunt one of these side streets, where the gondolas come rarely, and the tourists never.

"Diana." His voice surprises me, dark and low in the shadows. "Come back to bed."

In bed, often, he will call me his goddess, his little moon. Diana has always been my favorite of the mythical figures, the huntress, the virgin, the wild one who goes forth alone.

My baby had no name. We promised we would wait to name her until she arrived, until we could see her little face. She came sooner than we thought. I wondered why my water didn't break before the pains began. One moment I said I wanted natural childbirth and in the next I was attached to monitors, needles sinking into my skin. In my mouth I tasted steel.

Perfectly formed she was when they pulled her out, and perfectly still, skin veined and clear as a jellyfish, fingers curled like tiny tentacles. No breath stirred the buttoned mouth. Dead *in utero*, the doctor said, at least a day. They covered her little wrinkled anemone face, put a blanket over her and took her away. They would not let me hold my daughter in my arms just once.

Gary walked beside the bed as they wheeled me to a private room. He knotted his fists in my bedgown and sobbed with an open and uncomplicated grief. I turned my face to the wall, a marble, a stone. I did not weep. My milk never came in, though my breasts ached. My body turned into a tomb.

He doesn't hear me leave the room. Down the stairs, out the door, with no more than my nightdress I am safe, independent. Free. And alone.

I leave my purse in the room; perhaps I don't mean it. I just want to see what the world looks like at night, without knowing if Gary will come for me. The air feels different from the warm heavy mass of the day, light and cool and sharp, the outlines of buildings and trees are as clear as though incised in glass.

I could go back to St. Mark's, join the throngs of people strolling or drinking wine along the Grand Canal, nameless among the crowd. In the side canal beneath our window there is no traffic; it is too shallow for boats. A mysterious scent follows me, swirling like the hem of my nightgown around my calves.

My life before Gary feels so far away now. I couldn't work again at my mother's shop, making alterations, living each day under her accusing eye, an open failure. I cried when we watched the sunset from the top of the Arc du Triomphe. The people in their cars circling the roundabout, beeping their horns at each other, so busy with their lives, so unmindful of being observed. How did they deserve that freedom? Gary handed me his handkerchief and drew my head onto his shoulder. He pointed out the clouds making bands of purple and persimmon across the sky.

The paving stones are cool under my bare feet. A window box above me blooms with moonflowers, opening only in darkness. I stop to touch the iron fluting on the rail of the bridge and see the name carved into a square of the walk, captured before the cement had time to set. In the dim light I crouch to make out the letters. MARIA.

Now there's a name to carry with you: Holy Lady, Queen of Heaven, Mother of God. It captivates me suddenly that Maria was here. I imagine her, dark hair flying behind her, mischievously squatting and tracing out her name with a stick or her fingers. No other name, no hearts or arrows or frills, just her, proud and wild and alone.

I want to find something sharp and put my name next to hers, just to prove that I have a presence, a hand that can cut stone. I long for the cement to be wet again so that we can both be inscribed there, so people next week, and next year, and years after, until the bridge collapses or the canal dries up completely, can walk between these buildings and see our names.

Let them wonder when Maria was here, and where she went afterwards with sticky fingers, if she left to raise a brood of children or if she ended up with her bones at the bottom of the sister sea. Let them wonder if Diana went to her husband to try again or if she left him, slipping down a side street, sliding over a bridge. They would never know, of course, but when I trace my fingers, very carefully, over the worn and engraved letters, I feel the sense that Maria is at peace.

At the next church I will light a candle for her. Somehow, it will be enough.

The steps creak gently as I climb them again. The room I enter is subtly different than the one I left. The slant of moonlight falling through the window is not the same as that on the street below. That may or may not be my husband with his tousled head on the pillow, his eyes squinted shut with sleep. There might yet be a Diana outside, walking steadily away, with no destination.

The sheets are cool again and the sweat has dried. Gary draws me close to him and rests his hand on my belly, still a hard little lump. Once, as a child, I thought I could swallow a watermelon seed and grow the fruit inside me. Now I wonder if anything will grow there again, if my body has already begun to decay.

I look at my husband's hand, the long warm fingers, splayed over my middle like a starfish on a rock. I could pick it up and hold it against my heart. I could just let it lie there and hope the warmth began some deep conjuring that would make my womb open and cleanse the debris. Or I could push the hand aside, but I imagine, if dislodged, it would simply drift away, floating on the tide, to wash up on another shore and perhaps rest there for a while, gleaming like an unnamed headstone under the moon.

Sudden Gone

A GIRL IS WALKING crooked down a sidewalk, indigo sky, skin itching like a hunger. Think you know this story? Streetlamps bending convex like a pearl, starlight underneath a fingernail. The girl is eighteen and leaving a party where her love showed up with another girl, Barbie-doll blonde. The girl is twenty-two and weaving drunk, just fought with her boyfriend, her mother. A car—red, sharp and clean—leaps the curb fast as a blade and kills her instantly. Body flies and drops like the bottom of a tunnel, the zoom from far away outdistancing the surprised sweep of blood. The girl is nine years old.

For months afterward, every car bumper in the neighborhood, in solidarity, sported a blazing pink sticker that asked, "Where's Deirdre?" Where's Deirdre, as though she were a stray wandered off full-moon and daring, would trail home matted hair scratched skin smug smile with a secret behind the lips. Bright pink, mind you, bunny girl pink, little pink, birthday pink. Like she had just stepped down the street for bubble gum and not come back. Like the driver would dare come through that town again and the guilt would kill him.

Actually she hadn't fought with her mother. It's true her mother had little time, always Ann Taylor in pressed skirts, typed briefs and client meetings, numbered to-do lists Monday morning magneted to the fridge. True Deirdre didn't like her mother's smell and thought of cats, damp moss, that corner of the basement where the drain sank into the concrete and she imagined it plunged down deep, through murky layers of stone and soil where things slithered and quested in the dark, drove straight through to the burning molten center of the world and every once in a while, when no one was looking, an ancient question would bubble up frothed with lava smoke. Deirdre avoided that drain like a crocodile might come out of it. Child's fears. She wouldn't have told her parents about the things she saw down it, leagues below the surface.

But memory, that traitor, that worm, will cast up its blind pink eye and knit a family, forge a communal closeness, cast a steel bond that turns tragedy into a Winnie-the-Pooh paint-by-number, a flat of contrasts. No dimension, no shadow. Behind closed doors it's no one's business, that's why we build houses and shutter the windows. The stories, the real ones, go down deep as that drain where Deirdre thought sometimes the devil might be listening. Answers stay buried like bones, pressed stones among the smudged damp layers and the things that slither.

Where's Deirdre? There are no answers. There are no reasons. There is a flash of energy, of exuberance, of brilliance or ecstasy or despair, and then the wick is cut and the candles go out. All that lingers is the Cheshire-cat smile, the line-up of blue-backdropped grade school pictures, glasses acne braces bad hair. In the Lindemann's yard the lawn ornaments with their blank metal smiles perpetually watch the street where their daughter disappeared. The paddles of the windmill move, full circle round, one following another, year after year turning their faces up to the sun.

Table for Four

THE MUZAK VERSION of Patsy Cline's "Crazy" came over the sound system for the fourth time that evening. Doris passed through the grid of booths and tables, carrying an empty coffee pitcher, eyeing the level of drinks in glasses and the progress of eaten meals. Her padded soles made no sound on the carpeted floor.

She was invisible to the diners, drifting through their low-voiced conversations and self-conscious laughter, no more to them than the gleam of reflected light on the windows, the framed prints and frilled curtains with their tiny film of dust. It felt to her sometimes, in the middle of an evening rush like this, that she alone held the secret that animated this little restaurant, she alone had the hawk's-eye view of its organization, its beating heart, and if she forgot the secret, if the knowledge went from her, everything around her would disappear.

Doris pinched the bridge of her nose, muting the throbbing in her head. She stepped through the swinging doors into the kitchen to see Tina leaning against one of the prep tables, knees crossed, arms folded over the front of her regulation white apron, chatting to Bert, the cook. Across the room, Harry hovered before the pastry oven, his hands pasty with powdered sugar. Tina tossed her dark ponytail over her shoulder and continued her account of her prior evening.

"So we go dancin', you know that place by the river, and he buys me a couple a drinks and such."

The waitstaff's corporate-issued uniforms were as prim as a restaurant advertising itself as family-style could be, but Tina managed here and there to add a sexy touch, wearing pantyhose with the seam up the back and cinching her apron as tightly as would still allow her to breathe. Doris tugged, not lightly, on one black curl.

"Oh, Tina, this story again? I think I heard it eight times already."

Doris ripped four pages off her pad and clipped them to the order wheel with one hand while with the other she tapped the spigot on the industrial-size coffee brewer and released a stream of regular, then decaf. She clicked a fingernail against the beeping timer to silence it. "All right, how long's this alarm been going off?"

Tina and Bert watched her, unimpressed. Doris sighed. "Never mind that I've been working this restaurant for over twenty years," she began.

"—and gone through seven changes of ownership, we know, we know." Tina rolled her eyes. The bracelets on her wrists jangled as she unclasped her arms. "Dory, I heard *this* story eight *hundred* times."

"And you been working here five months, so you know the coffee gets two hours," Doris said. "Two hours! Burn the coffee and they'll all go down the street to the truck stop."

"So you went out dancing," Bert prompted as Doris's stiff back moved past them in the direction of the dining room. Doris whirled around.

"Want to know how it ends?" she barked, coffee hot in her hands. "He takes her home, and he wants to come in. And she acts all surprised, like she's not wearing that red lipstick and a skirt up to *here*—" She angled one stiff hand at her waist, a ridiculous presumption and she knew it—"so he tries to grope her and she kicks him out, and he's coming in at seven and she's not gonna talk to him and you're gonna be stuck in the middle, got that?"

Bert shuffled back to the grill, scratching at the blue

bandana on his head. Tina moved to the coffee maker and yanked at filters and reservoirs. Doris looked at their blue-uniformed backs, shutting her out like the evil stepmother. This was why she told Joe she didn't want kids.

"That's medium on the steak, El Greco. Medium, not medium rare. Mess up the steak and they'll all—"

"Yeah, yeah, go cross town to the steakhouse," Bert chorused, whacking the top of a prime rib fillet with his spatula. Juices hissed along the scalding surface. "And I'm Puerto Rican!" he yelled at Doris as the doors swung shut behind her. "Ro-*bert*-o, got that?"

"Jeez, Dory, what crawled up your butt?"

Tina hissed as Doris finished a round of refills, following her back to the warming plate. Doris snapped a smile on her face for the benefit of table sixteen, her older couple sipping at their orange juice and squabbling over whether the dumplings had been too dry last time, or too doughy. She saw these people and others like them all day, every day, yet tonight every party she served held menace.

This couple could be her and Joe in twenty more years, sick to death of each other and terrified of the alternative. The four divorcees sharing dessert at table twenty could be her and her friends if Joe ever left her. She looked at Tina's girl's smooth face, the only lines around her eyes made by pencil, her skin as soft as the whipped cream on one of Harry's pies.

"Why these cooks, Tina? They're boys. They're sweet, but they don't know anything about the world, about women. Is it just because they're Latino and your mama don't care who he is as long as he's not white?"

Tina pouted, sticking out a lower lip lined with a berry color one shade darker than her lip color, a startling line of division. "You don't know how it is, Dory. In this town? You already got Joe."

"Joe!" Doris bit off a laugh; it sounded bitter. "Look, if he calls me on the manager line, tell him I can't talk."

Tina waited wide-eyed for an explanation, but Doris turned away. Her eyes flicked to the front of the restaurant as a trio of women set off the courtesy chimes. "I'm too busy, that's all. Where is that hostess girl?"

Tina flipped a handful of black curls over her shoulder and sighed as Doris's straight shoulders retreated. Doris advised everyone else on their personal lives but clammed up about her own.

Marching to the front register, Doris saw the street lamps in the parking lot flicker on and risked a look at the clock above the bakery counter. Five thirty. *Damn daylight savings time.*

Beneath the reinforced counter glass, twelve-hour-old muffins and cinnamon rolls sagged against the sides of their platters, sugar glaze congealing on their tops. Harry, huddled over the pastry oven in the back, would bring out a sheet of crème pies and apple tarts in a moment or two, and soon the night shift would drift in to help with the dinner-hour traffic. Doris resisted the urge to calculate the tips she had collected so far. She resisted the urge to think about Joe.

She smiled at the waiting women while she rang up a tab. "Someone'll be right with you."

A mother and two daughters, the girls' faces maturing into the mother's dark eyebrows and long nose. They stood without moving, expressions vacant, waiting for direction. Where was dad? Doris wondered. Gone? Abandoned, booted out for cheating his wife or his company? Just decided he didn't want to be there anymore, threw down his tools and walked off the job?

Doris felt a sharp pain in her wrists as she stabbed at the register buttons. She might be developing tendonitis. *Joe, after twenty years? How could you do this to me?*

The mother turned to one of the girls. "Are you sure about this?"

"I'm all right," the girl answered, looking in the opposite direction.

The bells on the entry doors rang at the same time as the cash drawer, and dad stepped in, middle-aged, wearing a heavy winter jacket and a logoed cap. Out to celebrate a minor triumph, or dad just decided he'd spring for a good square meal when mom declared she didn't want to cook.

Yet she knew them, Doris thought; she could see in the way they stood a certain strangeness with one another, the subtle but huge distances between people who nevertheless shared their lives. All of them floating together on separate life rafts, in the same sea.

Doris jumped as Jenny, the hostess, appeared at her elbow, tiny, smiling, blonde. "Four tonight? Booth or table?"

"Booth," the mother answered for them. She glanced again at the daughter on her left, a look betraying its mark of preference. Jenny smiled and led them away, plucking four menus out of the box.

Not my section, not my section, Doris hoped. She didn't want to have to wait on these girls who could have been her own daughters. Didn't want to think what she'd said no to when now, as never before, the choice might be taken away for good.

She guessed that the girls were in college, a year or two apart; they might be twins, except the one was so much thinner than the other. The first girl, the one the mother had not looked at, sported the universal collegiate uniform, a shabby pair of jeans and a hooded sweatshirt broadcasting the nearby state college across the front, a little frayed at the sleeves. Ponytail and beat-up sneakers, this girl was paying her own way now and couldn't afford much.

Her sister was too lazy to get dressed or subscribing to some fashion trend that Doris hadn't seen yet; she wore black leggings with a long sleeved green shirt, the color of army issue, and a blue bandana over her head. Her slip-on loafers, looking like felt bedroom slippers she might have borrowed from her grandfather, scuffed across the geometric maroons and purples of the carpet as Jenny led them to table ten and dealt out the menus. *Damn.*

Doris watched them as she dropped the tab on the table of the older couple, knowing they were as anxious to leave as she was to move them. They tipped like it was still 1950 and they were at the downtown soda fountain.

The mother and sweat-shirted daughter flanked the other girl like a rear and advance guard, waiting for her to sit down before they took their places. The baby, Doris supposed. The favorite. The bold, outspoken one who got away with things because she was spirited and clever. Probably the ponytail girl, the average girl, the student and the athlete, still got told to sit up straight.

Doris had been marked in the same way, growing up in the shadow of a charming sibling who worried their parents to impatience while Doris, steady smile on her face, never worried anyone. She wondered what Lydia was doing right now. Joe complained about how much time she spent on the phone, but Joe had been an only child.

Fetching water glasses for her new table, Doris saw that the pitcher was empty and seethed. These kids!

They never paid attention to anything, too busy flirting with each other, complaining about their lives. Doris herself wouldn't be working here if she had other options, but she never saw that complaining did anyone any good.

She'd had her dreams once, too. The photo shop she worked in after high school, when she wanted to be an actress, until she appeared in a publicity spot on a local channel and saw what she looked like on-screen. Now she acted all the time, every shift.

In the kitchen, Tina coached Bert on his behavior for when Julio punched in. "Don't talk to him, all right? But tell me everything he says about me. And don't believe him if he says—you know—anything happened. Okay?"

"Doris!" Harry yelled from the manager's office, brandishing the cordless in his hand. "Phone for you! Joe."

"Not on your life!" Doris rapped out. "I'm in the middle of a rush here." She ignored Harry's surprised look and moved to the ice maker.

"Trouble with Joe," Tina whispered, loud enough so everyone could hear her over the roil of the dishwasher, the thrum of the freezers and the hiss of the grill, even the blare from the TV.

Doris poked at a button and let the rumble of the ice machine drown out other sounds. Tina said *Joe* like he was some TV personality rather than the plain, heavy-set man who'd been living in Doris's house and sleeping in her bed for—well, half her life.

"Yeah, everybody's got problems," Bert said, jabbing his metal spatula toward the screen. On it, a camera jounced over the rubble of mud-baked buildings and zoomed in like a rifle sight on the fleeing forms of dark, bearded men in robes.

"See that?" Bert growled. "Two more troops killed

in Afghanistan today. Two more."

"How many now?" Tina asked, moving closer. "In Iraq, I mean?"

Doris grabbed her water pitcher and fled before she could hear the answer.

She wondered what Joe wanted to say to her as she reeled off the night's specials to the family of four. He'd been complaining about the foreman on his new project and Doris knew he was just itching to start a row with the man, who was younger and had been on far fewer sites than Joe had. No use pointing out to Joe that he never got put in charge of sites because he never got along with anyone, always thought somebody was out to stab him in the back or discredit him in one way or another.

Doris tallied in her head the bills they couldn't pay if Joe got fired from yet another job. There'd be no fixing her car, they'd be late again on the utility bill, and what it would do to his Social Security, she didn't even want to imagine. The thought made her veins hurt, deep underneath her skin.

She jotted down their drinks: coffee for dad, just water for mom, a flavored iced tea for the ponytail sister. They all looked expectantly at the smaller girl. She leaned over the menu and fidgeted with her jewelry, first the silver bracelet looped over the bones of her wrist, then what looked like a shoestring draped around her neck, descending below the open buttons of her collar, hiding the pendant.

"Tomato juice," she said in a quiet voice, looking up.

Doris felt a jolt as the dark eyes met hers, large and liquid. She'd seen those same eyes on the deer her father used to bring home during bow season, their soft eyes frozen open in fright. The girl's face was nothing but skin, sallow in tone, netted over the jutting bones of her face. Doris glanced at her hands as she folded her menu and realized the silver ornament on her wrist was an ID bracelet, the kind given to people with a medical condition.

"Large or small?" Doris asked, hearing her voice hitch.

"Small," the girl said after a moment.

"Large," the mother corrected, looking covetously at her offspring. "Just try, honey."

The mother repeated the specials as Doris turned away, as though she thought her daughter might not have heard, or might be tempted by the thought of chicken and dumplings if mentioned a second time. Pausing by the next booth to see how everything was tonight, and did they need anything else, Doris heard the elder sister chirp, "Well, it has to be better than hospital food, right?"

"No, she did really well today," the mother said, with the stern cheerfulness of a reporter. "She ate the Jell-o, and part of the chicken—oh, then you don't want chicken again, do you honey?"

"I said *medium*." The man at Doris's elbow glared at her. "This is medium *rare.*"

"I'll get you another," Doris said, sweeping the plate out from beneath his nose, half-eaten mashed potatoes and all. "Just a few minutes."

"Maybe you need to explain to that cook the difference between medium and medium rare," the man said, snapping back his fork so he could finish his vegetables. "Think he speaks enough English to understand that? Don't they have salmonella in his country?"

"You know, I keep telling the manager we should have a deal with the hospital," Doris said coolly, pocketing her order pad with her free hand. "Something where we get kickbacks if we send them people with food poisoning. They're only a few blocks away, you know." She patted him on the shoulder, rudely.

"Is your manager here now?" the man called to the back of Doris's apron, but she swept away as she heard laughter rising from the table for four behind her. There was something spooky in it, like canned laughter, forced and artificial. Parents laughing at a kindergarten play, a little embarrassed at their child's clumsiness, a little afraid of what they might turn into.

She banged through the swinging doors to the kitchen and put a hand over her heart. She was the best with irate customers. She always sent them home smoothed-over and happy. What had come over her tonight? That girl's ID bracelet? They had hospital patients in here all the time, celebrating their release with a solid meal. But from the way the family talked, it didn't sound like the girl had been released.

"Doris?" Jenny emerged from the manager's office, her face gleaming prettily in the kitchen steam. "Joe called for you. He said he's on his way home."

"He got fired again, I just know it." Doris slapped down a drink tray and grabbed at a handful of glasses. "I told him if he got fired, don't bother coming home."

Jenny stared. She'd been dating the same boy for three years now, Jim or Jack or Johnny his name was. She wore his letter jacket and he bought her flowers before all the school dances. Jenny agonized to Doris over college applications, what might happen if they got accepted to separate places. She had her heart set on the Baptist college but he had been offered an athletic scholarship to the state school and Doris counseled them both, remembering how easy it had been for her and Joe, how they just started hanging around together and then didn't know how to be apart. Doris nagged and Joe grouched but they had never split. She had never, ever threatened to kick him out.

Bert stared, pulling at the knot in his bandana while gunfire bloomed on the TV above him. Joe and Doris were two indissoluble names to Bert, the signifiers of a legendary America, like Lucy and Desi, like apple and pie.

"Hey Ro-*bert*-o, I told you that guy at seventeen wanted his cut medium, not medium rare. He thinks you're trying to give him salmonella or something."

"You don't get salmonella from beef," Bert howled. "And that *was* medium. He's getting well done if he can't tell the difference."

A hiss of fresh juice leapt from the grill as Bert threw on a steak, wreathing them all in meat-scented vapor. Bert sweet-talked all the waitresses, even Doris, but he was serious about his work.

"Dory, you all right?"

Tina stroked the golden pendant she usually wore tucked beneath her apron. Doris studied the small cross, thinking of the icons she'd seen taped to the dash of Tina's car, the rosary dangling from the rearview mirror. Tina walked around in a cloud of protection, ringed by a warm steam of prayer.

"Ah, I'm fine," Doris said, spilling a stream of tomato juice half into, half out of the glass. Had the girl ordered a small or a large? Damn it, she couldn't remember. "I have a hospital patient at ten," she admitted. "It just cuts me up when we have the sick kids in here."

Tina patted her arm gently, then lifted a large tray crammed with dinner plates. "It'll be okay, Dory. Don't you worry about Joe."

As she approached the family's table, Doris felt herself slowing down, moving more carefully, reluctant to upset the fragile contentment between them as they talked idly to one another. The girls reminded Doris of her and Lydia, though she and Lydia never looked so alike. The healthy one sat slouched forward, elbows on the table, building castles with packets of sugar substitute and non-dairy creamer, while her sister sat with quiet hands and her shoulders bowed inward, as though shielding her heart or responding to some chronic inward pain. They seemed more a shadow version than a mirror image of the same person, the one a finer replica of the other, her limbs fragile with their lack of excess flesh, her features made delicate by the luminous pallor of her face.

Doris passed out the drinks and the girl's face fell as she saw the glass of red-blood liquid before her. "Oh, I wanted small," she said.

"My mistake," Doris said. "I won't charge you for it." She averted her eyes as the girl turned her face toward her, looking instead at dad. "Ready to order?"

She scribbled automatically as they spoke, remembering how she had watched Lydia in school chorus and later in community plays, singing her heart out and mugging for the camera, while Doris, quiet, complacent, clapped dutifully in the audience. Lydia ran away long ago and was living with some playwright in New York, trying to be the actress Doris never was, as though putting herself in front of a camera, clothes on or off, was acting.

Anything in public was acting, Doris thought. Here were four people out having dinner, just like the scrubbed and healthy actors the restaurant chain hired for their commercials. Presenting a normal, well adjusted, façade to the world, saying and doing all the accepted or expected things, the whole time leading inner lives filled with quiet rage.

They were waiting, again, for the girl. "You can take more time if you need it," the mother said.

"There's no rush. We're on pass."

It was as though they spoke a coded language or didn't expect her to understand, Doris thought as she waited quietly. She was an outsider, part of a hostile, germ-infested world.

She wondered what was wrong with the girl. She heard that same ache in her own voice when her sister called, or when she said goodbye to Joe on the mornings he didn't look at her, packing up his lunch and hard hat and safety goggles as though he were going far away.

She studied the girl's face, fascinated by her uncanny thinness. She was like some wild delicate creature, an ibix maybe, trapped at the zoo, something precious and rare, almost too fragile to survive. No wonder her eyes looked so large; she barely had any eyelashes. Her eyebrows were almost non-existent. Beneath the wild paisley-print scarf tied around her head, small patches of stubble showed above the girl's ears.

"What was the soup again?" the girl asked, and Doris felt her heart drop when those dark eyes met hers again. For a moment she couldn't remember.

"I thought it was chicken dumpling," the mother said. Doris nodded, unable to speak.

"I'll have that," the girl said. "Just a cup."

Doris nodded and scribbled. She was forgetting herself, forgetting what she was supposed to do here. She wanted to put her arms around the girl. She wanted to hold her delicate hairless head against her chest and weep.

"Anything else?" Doris asked brightly. The family demurred. She gathered up menus and fled.

In the kitchen, Julio whistled, tying his apron. Tina, filling a filter with ground coffee, ignored him completely. Bert thrust a thick hank of meat under

Doris's nose, still sizzling, grill marks incised into flesh. "For the beef-eater. Tell him to cut it in small pieces or he might choke."

Tina adjusted the seams on her hose, drawing the men's eyes. Inside the manager's office, the phone shrilled.

"I can't get that!" Harry yowled from the pastry oven. "My tarts come out in thirty seconds!"

Tina turned and caught the look on Doris's face. "Dory! *What* is the matter?"

"What? Nothing," Doris said, wiping her cheeks with the corner of her apron. "Jeez, it's hot in here."

"We still have enough soup?" Jenny popped her head in to ask. "Or should I take it off the chalkboard?"

"Jessica! Get the phone!" Harry howled.

Jenny bolted. A second later, her blonde head popped back out of the office, looking apologetic. "It's Joe."

"I don't have time to take a call," Doris said, indicating the plate.

"You want me to take it?" Tina offered. "You need a minute?"

"It's this family," Doris said, swiping at her face. "Look at this girl. She'll break your heart." She pulled Tina to the window in the swinging doors and whispered. "Table ten."

"What's the matter with her?" Tina whispered back.

"I think she's a cancer patient. A kid that young? With cancer?"

It felt callous to put the girl on display, but this sort of thing had to be looked at, if quietly. Doris tried to collect herself. She saw a lot of people in here every day, all with their separate ills, their overwhelming problems. She had lasted through seven changes in ownership because she knew not to take things personally. Every one of her tables had to feel like she was there just to make them happy, and then she forgot them as soon as the door chimed shut on their heels.

"Dory, kids get cancer every day. Of course it's terrible, but it *happens*."

Doris felt the hot platter burning her fingers and shifted her grip. It would never happen to her. It would never happen to one of her daughters.

"Joe said to tell you that he didn't get fired," Jenny said at her elbow in a quiet rush. "He walked off the job."

"Oh, that's great," Doris groaned. "He won't get severance if he walks. He better not dare come home." She lifted a foot and kicked the door open, trailing the odor of grilled steak as she went.

She worked her other tables, filling drinks and fetching ketchup, but the family of four kept drawing her eye. The healthy sister told stories that made the dad laugh and the mom shake her head, stories that required several broad sweeps of the arms as illustration. The other sister merely smiled and watched, looking perhaps at what she had been before this thing entered her life, this disease that chewed diligently at her insides.

Doris ducked back into the kitchen to drop off an order and found Bert, in Tina's absence, chatting with Julio. Bert reached up and adjusted his bandana.

"Ah, Dory. I was just telling Julio how my grandmother had the cancer, twice in her breast, but now she has remission again and very healthy, you know? So people can live through the cancer." He looked appealingly at Doris, stroking his heavy gold crucifix.

"Joe's mother died of breast cancer fifteen years

ago," Doris said shortly. "She never had a remission."

Bert's face fell. He pushed plates over the counter to her, and Doris loaded her tray.

"Is that a crucifix?" Tina said, entering the swinging doors as Doris turned. She peered through the order wheel at Bert. "Can I see it?" she asked, drawing her own necklace out to compare.

The family looked up expectantly as Doris approached with their food. "Here we go," she said with the cheerful plaster smile, passing out the dishes. Slightly dry grilled chicken breast for mom, slab of beef with the drowning potatoes for dad, undercooked pasta doused with thick sauce and a handful of shrimp for the sister, and for the girl, the miniature cup of soup. Doris set a salad down between the two girls. "Anything else I can get you?"

The girl picked up a packet of crackers and tried to open it, then, failing, set it down. Her dad reached over, tore off the corner, and handed the packet back to her. She picked up her spoon and dragged it through the cup. A dumpling surfaced, and after it a circular slice of carrot. She looked at it, then poked it back into the liquid.

Everyone watched her. "Do you want anything else, honey?" her mom asked. Doris had been about to say the same thing. Dad tore open another packet of crackers, just in case.

"No, this is fine." The girl glanced around with a small smile. "It looks good."

Doris knew she shouldn't hover. She wished for a moment she could sit down at the table, study this family and learn who they really were. She didn't even know their names, but how would that help? Sometimes she didn't feel like Doris, herself or any other Doris, though that was the name inscribed on her plastic tag.

The phone rang again as she entered the kitchen, but now everyone ignored it. Harry topped pies with exquisite concentration. Tina leaned against the counter, chatting torridly with Bert, while Julio whistled and shelled shrimp. Doris imagined herself sitting in her dark house that night, in the staccato blue light of the television, listening to the phone in the kitchen ring and ring, and then stop.

When she returned to table ten, Doris met laughter. "How is everything?" she asked with a smile, looking from face to face.

Dad had all but polished off the beef, with a bite pushed to one side. Mom had peeled the skin off her chicken. The sister's pasta had disappeared. Two sauce-drenched pieces of shrimp sat poised on the girl's soup saucer, as though the sister were trying to build the girl back up, one morsel at a time. The soup had barely been touched.

"Is the soup all right, honey?" Doris asked. "I can get you another."

"It was good," the girl said. She looked at the undisturbed plate next to her sister. "You didn't eat your salad."

With a finger the older girl pushed the plate in her direction. "I got it for you."

The girl leaned forward, picked up her fork, and pushed the leaves of lettuce around for a moment. Her shirt dropped away from her neck, showing the shoe-string necklace. Doris knew she was staring but she couldn't stop. There was no pendant. The cloth strip help up a small tube about half the size of Doris's little finger, one end of it tightly stoppered with a plastic blue cap. The other end disappeared directly into her chest, the seal lined with translucent tape. Doris didn't have to look at the ID bracelet as it slipped forward. She knew what it said.

As she turned away she heard them trying to tempt the girl with the tidbits they had saved. "A shrimp? My chicken skin? A piece of dad's beef?"

When she went to refill the coffee pitchers the kitchen was, in a rare moment, silent. Harry had taken his cooling pastries up front. The boys joked back by the freezers, their voices echoing in the tight space. Doris stood for a moment, breathing in and out, watching the TV.

The national news had given way to local, and a reporter stood in front of the area high school, talking about the new science grant. She waited to see some glimpse of the construction site, but why would Joe's project be featured? What was disaster in her own life wasn't news to anyone else.

Doris put a hand over her heart. She wished for a moment that she had a necklace to finger, or even Tina's simple gold cross. She had seen an atrial catheter before, on Joe's mother. After the chemo failed, and the radiation failed, when her veins one by one began collapsing, the doctors had no other way to keep a line open for fluids, painkillers, the blood transfusions after yet another surgery. They put in the tube a few weeks before she died.

Doris remembered those painful visits, not knowing what to say to the sick woman as she sank and sank further, no more than a ragbag of bones in the white-sheeted bed, until finally—mercifully, they had said to one another—she was no longer in any pain.

"Dessert?" Doris asked a few minutes later, returning to the family's table.

The mother looked at her daughter. "Strawberry cheesecake?" the sister teased. "French silk pie? Brownies dripping with hot fudge?"

The girl winced. "I wish."

"That's all right," the mother said. "We only had

an hour's pass anyway. We have to be back before your next dose at eight."

The sweat-shirted girl, the one who had eaten all her pasta, who would put her sister on her back and run up a hill with her if she had to, looked at her watch. "We have a few minutes yet. We could swing by the mall. Or go to the bookstore. Wasn't there a book you were looking for?"

"I'm a little tired," the other girl said.

Dad caught Doris's eyes. "We'll take the bill."

Doris passed the girl unexpectedly as she went to the register to get change. The slippers scuffed out of the aisle that led to the bathroom; she moved slowly, supporting herself with one hand on the wall. Doris wanted to put out a hand but, suddenly afraid she would injure her—bruise her skin, or dislodge something—she pulled her hand back.

The girl moved like she was a hundred years old. The sister waited on a bench by the door, while mom stood at the cash register, holding dad's wallet. No doubt dad had left to pull round the car.

Doris moved behind the register and pressed the buttons. She felt like she had tendonitis over every inch of her. Even her scalp ached. It was just a small moment, the chance to say one kind thing, and she had missed it. She had the feeling that for the rest of her life—however long she had to carry the weight of it—she would wish she had touched that girl.

She handed the change to the mother, wondering what she could say that would not be cruel. *Have a nice night! Drive safe! Thanks for stopping by!*

The mother glanced at the window as headlights flashed, then started for the door. The healthy girl put a hand under her sister's arm as she pushed herself to her feet.

"Thanks for stopping by," Doris said out of sheer

reflex. "Have a good evening."

"You too," both girls said automatically, without looking at her, and Doris wanted to kick herself.

"Come again soon," she said, the only thing she could think of.

Only the sweat-shirted girl, holding open a door while her mother did likewise, glanced back at her. "We will," she said, but did not smile.

Doris watched until the rear lights of the truck blended into the traffic, headed toward the hospital.

Doris heard the phone shrilling in the office, the sound a long high sting, but she picked up the receiver to find a buzz of dead air. The news ended and it was prime time. On all of the popular sitcoms, actors bumbled through imagined crises, delivering zingers that made the canned audience howl with laughter and ducking to commercial just as the tension escalated.

"Hey, Tina," Doris called as she untied her apron at the end of her shift, hanging it up on its peg. "You need anything before I leave?"

To her surprise, Tina hugged her. "Take it easy on yourself, Dory. And on Joe."

Doris shook her head as she reached for her jacket. Tina, the maven of love advice? The girl's perfume lingered on her shirt.

Doris walked past the hospital on her way home and looked up at the square array of windows, some lighted, some not. She wondered which room the girl was in. She imagined the nurses connecting their machines to the tube in the girl's heart, starting the slow drip of toxic chemicals. Her chest burned at the thought. She pictured the mother and father and sister, standing or sitting around the room, waiting, watching. Wondering what to pray for.

She was not surprised to see Joe's blue truck sitting in their driveway, shedding flecks of mud and rust onto the pavement. She had guessed he would be sitting on the couch, beer in hand, watching the baseball game and thinking about his foreman, this kid who had gone to school for four years to supervise what Joe knew after thirty years of hard experience. Doris set her purse down on the kitchen table and went into the living room where the light from the television flickered across the dark carpet.

"Hey," she said softly.

He didn't look at her, but his hand tightened around the aluminum can. Joe loved baseball, the strategy of it, the slow calculations and the swift bursts of action. It was just how he made love. Doris watched him for an endless moment, the light glancing off the scars and ruts of his profile, the inchoate poetry of his face.

Joe hadn't wanted kids either, said he didn't have the patience, made the usual arguments about not wanting to bring one more innocent in the bloodied world. It had been a mutual decision. Neither of them wanted to be helpless before the suffering of another creature.

She took a deep breath and sat down, not in her armchair, but on the couch next to him. She felt him move briefly in surprise.

"Hey," she said again. "Joe."

Should she tell him she wanted to work things out? Did she want to?

"I been thinking, Dory," he said in his slow rumble. She listened and waited.

"We ain't perfect," he said. "But we got something. And something—" He still didn't look at her, struggling for the first time to define his personal philosophy—"is better than nothing."

"Oh, I know it," Doris said, reaching out for the warmth and smell of him, asphalt and engine grease and alcohol and earth. He slid his free arm around her waist and leaned his head into her shoulder, his hair flattened, his stubbled cheek scraping her fingers. How beautiful, Doris thought, the slow familiar orbit of habit and need, the struggles between hope and suffering; beautiful, that ache in her throat, life pressing out of her, a greedy thing.

She laid her hand on his head, a tender blessing. "I know it, Joe."

Someone in the House

SOMETHING IS DIFFERENT: something is not as you left it. The house holds a suggestion, a vibration only, a signal of danger pulsing like waves of cold air. The cold comes from the basement. The waves come from the window, leaning open like a drunk. Fear makes its fist in your chest. Wide open, fallen open, accidental open, this window, accessible from the ground, large enough to admit a body, the possibility of someone stepping into your basement, someone clad in black and carrying a crowbar, or a garbage bag, strange shoes padding over the cement floor, creaking up the stairs, this window has created an access point, a permeable space, a back door.

The potted plant, fronds mashed against a ceiling beam, wobbles in the cold air, shedding its dying leaves. No footprints. Reel quickly through the upstairs rooms: if anything is missing, anything gone. But the DVD player squats on the entertainment center, the stereo on the bookshelf, staring at you with serene blank digital faces, not their business to attract, the bottom-line digital equipment, the supermarket stereo, not their business to judge the movies you watch (the occasional romantic comedy, all right), the music to which you listen (sometimes high-pitched, occasionally operatic or sentimental). There is no one in the house, no one in your bed, no one has been in your bed, or your house, for many many many many months (except of course you and the cat), and there is also no lock-box in the house, no stock certificates, nothing of value, nothing (except of course you), and the bowl of spare change stands unstirred on your bedroom vanity, collecting dust, like all your spare things, like your vanity.

How did the window fall open like that? Anyone could have come in. Who could have come in? What did he want?

Push the window back in place. Push again. There is no lock.

The cement is cold; the air is cold, significantly cold, arctic cold, alone-with-nothing-moving-except-for-ions cold. Turn on the space heater. Pull on socks. Hide in bed, blanket over your eyes, ears awake to the grunt of the furnace as it rubs its iron insides. Someone has watched this place, knows your habits, knows you live alone and no one comes over, you are a single female, vulnerable, prey. He (bold, black-clad) has penetrated your space, looked at your things, perhaps even run his hands over your surfaces. Someone unknown to you has become intimately possessive of your possessions.

Leave the leaves where they fell, like brittle pieces of candy, like the crumbling leaves of a manuscript, like the leavings of a shipwreck. Too much effort to pick them up, piece by piece. The heater hums. Imagine the sound one more particle of dust makes as it settles, a pinprick, an atomic ping.

THE NEXT DAY: Tissues in the bathroom garbage. Suspicious. Red smears, like a nosebleed. Your nose has not bled since seventh grade, when it did so once and with sudden violence, while the short loud boy you were half in love with tried to sell you raffle tickets for the freshman dance. Whose nosebleed? Whose nose? You did remove toenail polish last night, chipped and chafing at the edges, bright red polish no one but you has seen, a lustful secret between the eleven of you, you and your toes. You did run out of cotton balls (must run to store soon). You did use tissue. Maybe.

Or, someone else's nose has bled into your Kleenex.

Check: medications are intact. Wonder who looked in here, looked at the labels, tried to imagine you, imagined being you opening the glass door and looking at rows of sleeping pills, anti-anxiety pills, aspirin, Lactaid, Rolaids, all the aids, the labels of sleeping pills and antidepressants facing discreetly inward, hiding their eyes, pursing their lips like old spinsters (all those bottles that you don't need, really). But you keep the labels out, do you not, using them to double-check against the calendar, the date and dose, the name of this day of the week which is all you have to distinguish it from the constant blur of other moments, other labels, other days, so who has been looking at your labels, who has been looking at your life?

NEXT WEEKEND, roll out of bed early. Shower. Dress. Put something in your hair, a clip, a ponytail holder, some type of accessory to indicate you are not entirely unconscious of appearance, you are not entirely immune. Go to the museum. Wander into unused corridors looking for dust. Avoid eye contact. Make a donation ($2).

Home: window closed. No one here (except of course you and the cat). Yet surely you did not leave a cheese slice wrapper on top of the garbage like that, did you or did you not have oatmeal for breakfast? When have you ever had cheese slices for breakfast, in this long and well-documented, quite familiar history of fixing yourself meals?

Someone was here. He was here. Note for grocery list: buy more cheese.

LATE AFTERNOON, the phone rings. Two shrill

ratchets, then a hang-up. No message. Maybe someone is trying to contact you. (To say what? You need to clean your toilet? You need more cheese?)

TWO DAYS later, footprints in the mud, leading next door. A man's prints, firm and deep.

Stack of mail for you. Still.

LATER IN the week: a dent in the bedspread, not there this morning. You made the bed, you always make the bed, otherwise the temptation is too strong to crawl back into bed, to call to work suddenly sick, ill, a friend on the point of desperation, a relative on the brink of death.

Cat, sleeping on chair, blinks at you. The sleeping chair is still warm from its body. Could have been cat on bed. Could be.

Lie down in dent, testing for a lingering warmth. Not warm. Too small for a human shape. Still.

Change the litter in the box. There must be no offensive odor to drive others away, including the cat.

That evening, alone, which is your custom, which is your preference, remember, dig out that old nightgown, now wrinkled, at the back of your dresser drawer, not worn since a long-ago boyfriend, rather tight across the hips. Wander through candlelit house, pausing before curtains; wonder at what angle, in what light, from what precise position you are visible, and how much.

NO ONE'S eating the generic cheese slices. Switch to brand-name.

PHONE RINGS. Dial tone. Hang up.

LEAVE THE heat turned up. Set the TV remote on the

coffee table. You want this to be a comfortable place. You want this to feel like a home.

Return to: an old workout video on top of the DVD player, bought eons ago, light-years ago, in the prehistoric days when DVD players were new, when there was that boyfriend. Yet you are certain that last night you watched *Frankie and Johnny* again.

A hint? A hint about the hips?

Or: somebody wants you. Somebody wants this life. Somebody wants the space you have made here, an open mouth, waiting.

PHONE RINGS. A pause—a man's voice. Hello? *Hello?* Wait—wait to be asked. In the pause there are several types of silences.

He wants to sell you new windows. Tight, weather-proofed, triple-insulated windows. Tell him you have new windows. Tell him you have all the windows you need. Hang up.

GO FOR a run. Avoid eye contact. In the park behind your house, far away down the trail, a man receding. A red cap. Could be. Could be.

Come home to: door unlocked. On purpose. You never lock on a run, too easy to imagine the key flying out of your shoe, falling into a pile of leaves or under a bush, leaving you to break into your own house, or call a locksmith (too embarrassed to ask the neighbors, and what would they do, except want to see inside the house, want to know why you are running?). Pouring water from the jug—didn't you just refill this jug? Didn't you just go to the store and spend fifty cents?— hear a creak upstairs. Top step.

Freeze.

Wait, water cold, heart beating. Condensation forms on your glass. Sweat cools on your forehead.

Footsteps descending, slowly.
Cat blinks at you from the bottom step, then yawns.
Still.

WHEN YOU leave for work, it is not light. When you return from work, it is not light. There are many shades and frequencies of darkness.

IT'S BEEN quiet in the house, quiet for months. No footprints around back. No unaccountable garbage. The nightgown sits, laundered, folded, unused.

It could go on like this, indefinitely. He is always the back of the head in front of you on the bus, the profile moving away from you in the grocery store. He is shy. He wants to be near you, but not be threatening, nothing fearsome, nothing at risk. You are gentle; you understand. Of course. Of course.

Still: in the dark nights, the passing of hours, every day waking to the same, only the slow cycle of pills emptying out of the bottle, then refilling, the level in the water jug going up and down, the heat bills coming into the house with return envelopes and leaving the house attached to checks. The candle holders sit empty of candles. The cat eats and sleeps and messes the litter. You understand; you do.

Still.

Gravel

THE WOODEN SIGN said Cabin Rentals. The letters had endured scorching heat, thunderous rainstorms, insect swarms, and the relentless bore of the salt breeze, yet there they stood, a stubborn etching, a well-worn shrine. The building showed quiet neglect. Planks of siding sagged into one another, furred with lichen and warped with moisture. The screen door hung aslant, large slashes tearing the mesh. Faded oaks trailed gobbets of Spanish moss over the toothed wooden shingles of the roof, gracious swag of eaves cupping the flat grey bowl of sky. Before, this had always seemed comfortable, a refuge. Now it was tired.

As she grasped her hand along the wooden rail of the stairs Manya felt a hard, dry splinter pierce her palm. She tugged at the projecting end and it broke, leaving a dark needle tucked beneath her skin.

Inside, the room smelled of seaweed, dark and salt-sticky. Out the window, small green brackenish things poked through dirty white sand.

Manya put the jagged splinter in the pocket of her jeans, smoothed her thumb over the reddening wound. "Hello?"

Maps tracing trail routes dripped from the walls of the rental office. Manya's boots scuffed the dirty floor. Open brochures advertised prices for cabins and primitive sites. Firewood: four dollars for a bundle of finger-thin sticks. Across the street, Tuesdays and Thursdays, meetings for nature walks led by rangers from the state park. Manya knew them, eager and trained, their pressed brown uniforms with the Florida Park Service patch on the sleeve, a cross between a military rank and a Boy Scout badge.

She studied canoe rental prices, restrictions on burning, a guide to the area's venomous snakes. The small silver dome of a bell stared at her beside the cash register. The plunger made a useless click.

The woman who emerged from the back room had a robust glow that made the place seem quaint rather than shabby. Her cinnamon hair showed a margin of embarrassed blonde at the part. A cotton button-down shirt over a tight tank top, she had the sunburned look of a healthy, athletic woman who had never learned how to use cosmetics but slapped them on now as a barricade against advancing age.

Manya rubbed her stinging palm on her blue jeans. She should have put on a clean shirt. She should have combed her hair. She looked neglected, too.

"Reservation?" The woman's voice held a rasp, from cigarettes or sea air. She glanced at the binder on the counter, flipped a page.

"Markova." Manya placed her backpack on the floor and waited. Pages riffled. The woman's look hit Manya on the chin, thin and narrow.

"Tourist?"

"Not anymore." She shouldn't need to explain this every time. The naturalization ceremony at seventeen, the tests and the solemn oath in the courthouse while the Girl Scouts dipped and swirled the flag. The university tried to charge her as an international student, though she'd lived in the country since she was five. She was tired of justifying her existence.

"Says here two adults."

Manya smoothed her hand along the seam of her jeans. "It's just me."

"Same price." She snapped open a receipt book.

Manya looked at the golden wedding band on the woman's finger. Tanned skin folded around it like protection. Beneath the metal, Manya guessed, the skin was stark white, like the underbelly of a sea-going creature that never saw light.

"The other . . . my . . ." She tried again. "He died," Manya said.

That look again, a quick swoop, not quite to the level of Manya's eyes. The woman's voice dropped a pitch, thick as syrup. "You poor thing. I'm so sorry." Her vowels opened at the end like wings. *I'm so sorr-ah.* The gull-eyes dipped to Manya's left hand, bare of ring or markings. The cotton shoulders gathered in a shrug.

"Need linens?" she said, scratching the paper.

"Yes." Manya bit her lip. She needed so many things.

"I'll bring 'em out before supper." Her host tore off a receipt and held it over the plastic-capped counter. "You *pore* thing."

"It was sudden," Manya said. "No warning. Just like that." She picked up her backpack and held the straps with both hands.

"Those are the worst," the woman agreed. She pointed east. "Last one on the left."

"You still have canoes for rental?" Manya handed her cash.

"Oh, honey, there's weather comin tonight," the woman said. "Didn't you see that *sky*?"

MANYA REGARDED the sky as she parked before the last cabin in the row and heaved open the hatchback. Sadie sailed out in a spatter of hot fur. The sheltie was just starting to lose her winter coat. She thrust her nose in the air, desperately sniffing. The sky was the color of the water was the color of the sea oats bending in the breeze. A watercolor by a troubled artist: Glowering Sky with Dog. Sadie charged into the gulf and kicked up a sheet of spray. The droplets sprang high and hung for a moment, turned slowly, then collapsed into the tide while the dog tried to bite them out of the air.

Manya had forgotten the sound of the ocean. That thrumming like an endless world-size heart, hurling the water onto the sand and then, repentant, taking it back.

The tent sat rolled in its factory sealed bag. Manya pushed it aside. They had talked, long ago, of tenting together, going deep into the woods. Interesting couples shared a hobby. Winter camping, trail camping, backwoods country wide open to just the two of them, tucked like turtles into their below-zero sleeping bag. He was a mountain boy, wind in the blood. He left the unused tent with her after that last calm discussion, when he walked down the long flight of stairs into nothing. He left everything behind.

She'd reserved the luxury cabin, the biggest they had. One broad room, a fireplace flagged with attractive grey stone, a deep couch facing the window facing the sea. A sink and more counter space than a restaurant. A door leading to the closeted bathroom, and stairs circling to the loft overhead. The smell of sawdust, motes drifting through the pine-damp air. A quiet mold on the inside of things, like regret.

Manya stood in the center of the room, falling into the forgotten pulse of the ocean. She listened for her heart, for what it was doing deep in there, but had no sense of it beating. Nobody thought about the heart and its steady work until, of course, it stopped working.

She wondered who had helped him, who had come around the corner of the locker room to find him stranded on the cold tile, one hand to his gasping chest. The shut row of metal doors slanting down around them. The email sent out to everyone said he hit his head on one of the wooden benches. The coroner's report noted the contusion, not contributing to death. She imagined his hands clenched into the fabric of his sweaty T-shirt, or perhaps covering his throat. And the person who found him thinking, oh shit, oh *shit,* this is the end of *my* nice normal day.

She wondered who had called Jeannette. His wife.

She stood yet in the center of the room, watching the clouds like a layer cake billow from west to east, when a sharp knock blew the door open. Upstairs, a thump as Sadie threw herself off the bed and slip-slid down the narrow stairs.

"Thought I'd bring em now. I got time." The cabin keeper wore grey slacks and a pair of muddy boots.

"Oh." Manya held out her arms for the bedsheets. The woman moved past her and set the folded items on the couch. Her eyes moved along the room, looking to see what Manya had brought to the place. Luggage, extra blankets, candles wrapped within them. Hardly any food.

"Y'all right?" Her eyes were grey, too, like the sky. An effect of living too long next to the ocean, where the wind could be cold through the winters. storms drawing the color out of everything, the idle boredom, the visitors leaving, always leaving.

"I'm all right," Manya said.

"What was it, then?" the woman asked.

"What was what?" Manya put a hand on the stack of linens. Already they bore a fine sheen of sea salt.

"Your husband. You said it was quick."

"Oh," Manya said. "Aneurism. Heart." Had she said he was her husband?

The woman put her hand on her chest, just as Manya had when she first heard the news. Checking. She'd held it there for the most of that day, skipping the class she taught, calling in sick to the testing site. She imagined Jeannette, now a widow, doing the same thing, perhaps right this moment at the wake in the funeral home, holding an arm across her chest as people filed by and collapsed against her. Tomorrow, during the funeral, there would be eulogies from astounded friends. He was so young, they would all say. He ran marathons. He had a strong heart, a many-miled heart. It should have gone on pumping in all its electro-hydraulic splendor for decades, millions more beats left in it.

He had called Manya once in a while, late at night. At first she didn't answer. In the messages it sounded like he was crying.

THE STORM HUNG in the sky all evening, waiting. Manya took Sadie for a walk. She remembered more sand, more wildness, more beach, but there was only a strip of nubbly gravel shielding the water from the bristle of sea oats along the embankment. Shells and pebbles swatched the sand, a tiny crunch beneath her feet. The musty smell like a basement, moisture so thick the air was viscous. She remembered the breeze clean and sharp.

Insects grated from the trees, rising and falling like waves. The sea moved toward her and the sky away, a dappled grey tabby streaked with dust. Sadie's hair stood straight with electricity. The thunder sounded like distant traffic, the dim row of cabin lights strung like pale bright shells along the shore. The sand was light oatmeal, shale spotted with bits of red and blue, stretching away into a moist fog. Any moment he might walk from it, arms full of driftwood for a fire, stepping from another world where his heart was still beating, a world where she had said yes.

A red, raised nimbus circled the tiny jag of wood in her palm, working its way in. He told her on their first date that he had gravel under his skin. Boyhood accident, a header over the handlebars of his bike. The road peeled layers from his hip and leg but his elbow hit first, driving small rocks deep under the epidermis. His parents, Christian Scientists, saw no need for doctors to tell them the debris was safe to stay there. It was earth-made material; the cells, living and dying, would push the foreign matter out.

But the elbow scabbed, then healed, and a bumpy, bubbly patch remained. Manya had liked the strange texture of it, the terrain of an alien planet. Skin beneath her fingers, but something else terrestrial deep beneath that. She was no biologist; she studied geophysics, the land with its features and fields and inevitable forces. She understood electromagnetics, thermometrics, the hydrology of his sweating body, the moving plates of his bones. The meteorology of their combined atmosphere, with its strange and unmeasurable currents.

Manya paused as Sadie sniffed a spot on the beach. The trees fretted, tossing up their branches. The rustling wind sounded like rain. Small leaves and bits of moss revolved through the air. The chant of the insects grew monotonal. The dog lifted her sandy muzzle and whined.

Manya grabbed a loose stick and pried at the small dome of sand. The scissored claw of a crab emerged first, then its body, upside-down. With the stick she flipped it over. It clipped to the side, leaving small mounds of sand in its trail, then paused, resting. It must have been suffocating, trapped in the small space it had fled for refuge.

He'd planned adventures for them, safaris in Africa, canoe trips down the Amazon. It was she who said they should date other people. He grew heavy in sleep, throwing his arm across her chest, pressing her deep into the blankets. His hands started to clutch. On the wall calendar he outlined in black marker the weeks she was gone for conferences or research. The gravel under his skin itched.

Jeannette was Catholic. She believed in insurance, checkups. His voice on the messages had the tone she'd heard when he called her name in his sleep. Deep in nightmares he muttered the Russian phrases he learned so he could phone her parents. *Hello. How are you. I am well, thank you. May I speak to Manya? Is Manya there?*

The storm broke when she was still half a mile from the cabin. The trees raged with wind and loose leaves swooped like bats. Tendrils of lightning struck and shimmered, magnified. Thunder rattled her teeth. Sadie streaked for shelter as the first cold drops fell and goosebumps blossomed on Manya's arms. The rain whirled to meet her, blurring the world like a dusty mirror. Raindrops bounced off her shoulders, her calves, the back of her neck, places that for a long while had been touched by no hand but her own. The rain dotted her skin in frantic code.

Manya closed her eyes and lifted her face, listening to the message being tapped into her. She was alive. The ocean swelled and roared as raindrops patterned its surface. She'd forgotten how it felt, the ragged desperation of it, the joy that caught in the chest. The man she had loved was dead, and she was alive.

AT THE CABIN, she toweled off and filled the kettle with cold water. Visiting hours were over. The room would be empty save for the chairs and flowers, the poster boards of pictures, his marathon medals and track trophies, the dried corsage from their wedding. Manya had been on a research semester in Brazil but she mailed a leaded glass cocktail set as a gift. A few weeks after the honeymoon, she received a thank-you card embossed with the wife's new initials. Graceful handwriting expressed their gratitude for the glasses, gave their new address. Much later Manya realized neither of them drank.

And then what? His wife would go home to the house they bought together. His parents would return to their hotel and pray. Jeannette would ask her high school friends to stay with her, the same women who had been her bridesmaids. She was not the type to spend nights alone. She would press her dress for the funeral the next day, set out her shoes, put Kleenex and aspirin in her matching purse. She would stay up late weeping, or staring dry-eyed at the ceiling, into a darkness so complete it silenced the terror.

Manya built a fire and unrolled the sleeping bag on the sanded floor. The kettle boiled. She wasn't required to fast, but she would anyway. She draped a cloth over a driftwood side table and set out her icons, her rosary, her prayerbook, the candles she had lit for him every night since the call. The air was too thick for thought. She watched the fire climb the stiff currents, bend itself in a plunging ballet.

He thought her work, her research came between them. He thought reasoned arguments would bring her back. In her family they arranged marriages, daughters matched with the nice sons of childhood friends. As mates they were kind, respectful, polite. They did not produce tempestuous declarations, tears and longings. From that first kiss outside out dorm room, the hurried embraces in the halls of her lab, she knew there was no way they fit together, him sweaty from basketball practice, her hands smelling of copper. He was a cowboy and she was Russian. They lived on different tectonic plates.

The phone on the wall rang. Manya dropped her rosary. She'd turned off her cellphone, no service.

Who knew she was here?

The phone rang again, and Manya approached slowly, surprised the power had not been knocked out. She lifted the black receiver. "Hello?"

"Call for you," the rental woman said, and Manya heard a series of clicks, then an uncertain voice, a woman's. "Hello?"

"Jeanette?" Manya said.

"Manya?" She sounded confused. Manya imagined her looking at the phone, frowning. She'd had a tiring day and would be fuzzy-headed from weeping. "You're at this number? I . . ." She trailed off. They never knew what to say to one another.

"How are you?" Manya whispered.

Jeannette started to cry. The sounds were quiet beneath the wind pounding the window, but Manya heard the small gasps for air. She felt a needle in her heart and wondered if that was what he had felt, except larger, a swell like the tide and then the startling burst.

"Are you coming tomorrow?" Jeanette asked between hitches.

"I hadn't planned to," Manya said.

A gulp, then a small high hiss, like the cry of a bird. "He would want you there."

Manya looked at the prayer candles, the three flames dipping and dancing in the currents of air. "I'll come if you want me," she said.

"It's so awful," Jeannette sobbed. "I had to buy him underwear. I bought my husband new underwear to bury him." That high, steady whine again. It sounded like a gale blowing in from the gulf. "His mother complained about the coffin I picked. She didn't like the silver handles. And he—Manya, it doesn't even look like him. They put him in so much makeup."

Out the window Manya watched the lightning streak between the upper banks of clouds, bands of dark holding the blinding flash. Manya pictured him in his navy suit, his face old beneath the embalming, all the clever tricks applied to dead flesh. He would not look like someone either of them had known, had touched every inch of.

"Everyone keeps talking about how *young* he is. How sudden. Looking at him to figure out—what I did to him. What I did wrong." Jeannette lost herself in sobbing.

In the fire a stick snapped its fingers, and Manya jumped. Outside, the trees howled and threw up their hands.

After a while, Jeannette quieted. "I found this number in his work planner." Manya heard her hoarse breathing. "He said he was going away with a friend."

He'd come here often with her, their getaway while she was in graduate school, he in training at the law firm. He'd proposed to her in a canoe on the river trail, the vessel rocking slightly as he knelt. The summer heat had itched her skin and tiny black flies tacked to her eyes and her sweaty neck. She closed her mouth when he asked her. The words knocking at her lips were nonsense rhymes her *baba* had sang to her, games she had played in the preschool of a village that no longer existed. He'd left and she'd stayed, with her lab and her St. Olga cross and her dreams in Russian, and she didn't have to go to races or office parties or American ball games anymore.

"I come here this time every year," Manya said. "He must have remembered."

A long silence, while the wind whined. "He's been calling you?" The voice tiny, spoken through a small point, far away.

Manya rubbed the raw swell of her palm over her

heart. "Once or twice," she said. "Just catching up. You know he is good—was good—at keeping in touch."

She stumbled over the tenses. Waited for Jeannette to piece things together, catch her in the lie.

"I don't understand any of this," Jeannette said, her voice faint, thin, weary. "Nothing makes sense. I feel gutted." A pause. "You should be there. For him."

Manya looked at the red furrow in her hands. "I'll come," she said.

She fixed lemon tea and stoked the fire and thumbed her rosary, stroking the old beads, the weighted tassels. The thunder roared and hurled itself across the gulf to the distant lands beyond. She understood what was required. Penance. A final goodbye. Confession, witness, and absolution, so Jeannette believed things were over. Would never know she had almost lost her husband again.

MORNING DAWNED light as a pearl. The sky held the same white tint as the sand, the sea grey as the sea oats. Manya found the crab. It had pulled its body a few inches from its hole and anchored its one claw into the sand, holding against the tide. With her foot Manya bunched sand around the carcass and wondered why no other animal had disturbed it. She couldn't have known it was dying.

She placed the stack of linens on the plastic counter at the rental office, floral side up. The woman wore the same button-down shirt. The blonde roots showed a wider margin, already reclaiming their own. She patted the top sheet gently.

"Storm keep you awake?" she asked.

"No," Manya said honestly.

"I guess everybody grieves different," the woman said. Her sharp eyes fastened on Manya's left ear.

"I found a crab on the beach last night," Manya said at the door. She stopped and looked up at the faded map of the Florida Gulf coastline. "It had one claw."

The woman watched her. "Stone crab," she said, as if she could still hear the foreign accent, as if Manya knew nothing about the United States, nothing about the deep and secret workings of the earth. "That's how they harvest them. It grows back."

"This one won't," Manya said. "It was dead this morning."

The man's shirt fluttered as her shoulders rolled, the ring on her finger winking. This woman wouldn't know how the heart could swell from all that was stuffed into it, hurt and anger, guilt and neglect, growing so fat and gluttonous and engorged that it burst open. What had he thought about in those last seconds? His wife, and his lie to her? Maybe it felt like pitching headfirst over the handlebars, that fiery burn as the blood rushed everywhere, spinning weightless in a moment of space, far from the safe warm hands of prayer.

Manya didn't have an answer. Why she had told him the date, made the reservation. Why, after all this time, she'd said yes.

A swallow-tailed kite dipped past the window, giving its lonely cry.

"It's not something you'd wish on anybody," the woman said.

Manya pulled the door shut behind her.

Sadie leapt into her seat in the back of the wagon and settled on the unused tent. Next to it sat the jar holding her real wedding present from Brazil: rainforest soil, for that trip they'd never taken. In five hours she would be there, file into St. Mary's with everyone else in their quiet shades of black. There would be beautiful words, tears and flowers, solemn ritual to surround the magnificent blankness of death. Manya would stand with Jeannette next to his grave and say the words she'd owed him for a long time. They would fall the way the rain pockmarked the ocean, brief and then disappearing, bubbling like gravel under an elbow it had once been hers to kiss.

Manya turned the car north, toward the highway, toward the priest and the quiet confession. Behind her the horizon of sea stood empty, blank and still. She looked at her hand and saw that the skin of her palm had closed over the splinter, encasing it as in glass. She would carry it with her, a memory made flesh. If she could not be forgiven then at least she, too, would be marked.

The Last Word

TOM'S PICKUP IS alone in the parking lot when I turn in, skating over hard-packed gravel and snow. Not even the hard drinkers are here yet, the ones who come directly to the bar from shift change.

Tom and I have been Pete's customers since we were twelve. Tom's old man would bring us here drenched in the dirt and stink of hot days planting or haying or detasseling corn and tell Pete to crack us all a cold one. Pete would snap open two Coke bottles that numbed our fingers while Tom's dad downed an Old Milwaukee in one long, steady pull.

"Pe e's," the sign blinks at me. The new owner's name is Sean.

Dull neon gleams from the bare lumber walls and exposed ceiling. The bar is sticky with too many coats of polyurethane.

Tom sits with elbows splayed and back hunched, two empty glasses before him. Either he clocked out early or never showed up at all. I know his foreman and the man only gives a sick day if something is bleeding or removed.

"She left me," he says, looking straight ahead. "She walked out. Jess is gone."

I reach for a stool and sit down next to him, hard. "What?" I should try to sound surprised. "When?"

"Tuesday."

"The night of the storm?"

She hadn't come to my place. I've checked my cell phone; there are no texts. Maybe she meant it. It really was over. All of it.

"Beer's on me, man," I tell him.

The bartender slides over the glasses without peeling his eyes off the game. The head of my beer swells and foams down the side.

Was it four years ago or five that I helped Tom get fitted for a tux, rehearsed my toast in the church office, patted my pocket every ten seconds to make sure I hadn't dropped the rings?

It was a stupid speech. I don't remember a word of it, but it made Jess cry.

Tom hasn't gotten any sleep since Tuesday. His eyes are bloodshot, the dark skin beneath them veined like a jellyfish. He hasn't shaved.

"It was stupid," he says. "Something so stupid I don't even remember."

Two weeks ago we won the dart tournament here, punching new holes in the poster of the too-tan Budweiser girl. There she is now, all hair and cleavage and smooth legs, like no woman in this town.

Jess and Tom brought their own darts, metal-tipped. Sheila just smiled and hopped up on a bar stool to sip her beer. Jess drank rum and Cokes, hugged Sheila after each bull's-eye, high-fived everybody and called them "luv."

"Just another fight, right? I told her to get out. Last thing I said to her. Get out. So she got in her car and left."

"She'll come back," I tell him, which I don't actually believe, but it's what you offer in this moment. Because what else is there? It seems obvious: things die, are lost, get broken, go away. They just do.

Tom wipes a hard hand across his mouth, button missing on his flannel sleeve. Jess wears that shirt to go blackberry picking.

"Sure she'll come back. But I'll just toss her ass straight out again."

He shouldn't talk like that. Anyone else would believe him.

*

THREE WEEKS LATER Tom's at the grocery store, pushing a wobbly cart stocked with a bag of oranges and two cases of beer. This store's been here for longer than we've been alive and every item is always stocked in the exact same place, but Tom looks like he just landed in Fiji.

"So, she call yet?" I ask him, which is the same thing I asked him yesterday.

Used to be when I saw Tom out the window of my office, walking across the factory floor with our old buddies, he'd lift a hand and wave. It was the same wave he'd give from the floor of the gym when it was overtime with tied hoops, the same wave from the sodden football field when he was put back in fourth quarter to score the winning field goal. Last time I walked into Pete's he turned like he didn't even recognize me.

He shakes his head and takes a jar of spaghetti sauce from the shelf.

"Who knows where she is. She's not at her mother's. Her sisters haven't heard a thing. I've tried all her friends, even the one in Phoenix. I've blown up her voicemail. It's like she's trying to hide."

They're fighting again, Sheila said that night after darts. She stared at herself in the mirror, rubbing lotion onto her smile lines while I brushed my teeth.

So? I said. They always fight. That's just what they do.

After she went to bed I realized I'd better hide the box of condoms. Sheila's on the pill.

"Listen, you want to come over tonight? You can play cards with me and Sheila or something."

Tom shakes his head, rubs a hand over his growing beard. All Tom ever had to do was smile at a girl: the clarinet player in eighth grade, that hot baseball manager in the summer league.

Then Jess came to cheer for the visiting team our sophomore year and no other girl existed. We showed up at her school play, at her church, went to all her games until he finally got her number. There's never been anyone else for him, though I can't say the same of Jess.

It wasn't envy. It was never that. I was used to Tom having things I didn't.

"It's selfish, you know?" Tom says. "She has to know I'm going crazy here."

"She's trying to make you sorry," I say, because she probably is.

Sheila doesn't have a mean bone in her body, just this little adorable line that comes between her eyebrows when she says, "Andrew!" She gets cranky once a month, takes an aspirin and lies down, and that's it.

She came to town our first year of technical school and everything was different when the numbers were two and four. We have a new car and, since my promotion, payments on a house.

Tom chose to stay on the machines, grinding out cereal boxes. Says he likes the swing shift. Sheila teaches at the middle school and goes to Jess to get her hair done.

"Get all your bitching out?" I ask her when she nestles her head on my shoulder, curls soft and smelling like salon.

"Honestly, I don't know why she stays with him if he drives her so nuts." She sighs, then looks up at me and says, "I never bitch about you."

"I told her to call," Tom says. "Before she left. I told her to call. She said she would."

"She'll call," I say to the rows of canned beans.

*

WHEN THE DIVISION head tells me he let Tom go, I take a twelve-pack to the falling-down farmhouse Tom inherited when his old man died. He answers the door wearing sweatpants and a ripped T-shirt from our tech school days.

The place hasn't been cleaned in three months: laundry in the corner, newspapers on the couch. Their German shepherd howls from the back porch.

We sift through empty beer cans and frozen food trays to find the remote. Tom's wedding ring sits in one of the overflowing ashtrays.

"Jess sees this place, she'll kill you."

"She's not coming back." Tom punches the remote until the news comes on. "I told her it's over. Last thing I said to her. It's over."

I open two beers and hand him one. Tom's dish is down after the neighbor kid hit it with the snowplow, so we flip till we find some old NOVA show about insects.

We watch tarantula babies eat each other, then their mother. We watch a female black widow spider sink her fangs into the male.

Tonight I'll go home knowing the dishes from supper will be done and the bed will be warm with Sheila in it. I imagine Jess sitting in a cheap motel outside of Vegas, watching the phone and pulling up her hair.

All I can think is how shiny her hair was. Like a starry night in one of our clear summers, like a solid pitch coming straight over the plate, like that last light on the end of my street that means home.

"Will you look at that?" I say to Tom as we watch a female praying mantis tear off the head of the male after mating. "Maybe you're better off."

"Yeah," he says, popping another beer. "To hell with that."

*

THE POLICE CALL Jess's parents first, because it was their car. Her parents call Tom, and Tom calls me.

I go with him to watch the little Honda get hauled out of the creek bed a mile from our house. The fender is smashed, the front door missing. The Jaws of Life have already been in to cut Jess out.

Tom wants me to go with him to identify her body but I don't know if I can. We stand on the road together, sliced through by the cold of early April, and we say nothing.

There's a terrible gentle grace to it all, the crank of machinery, the heavy strength of iron and steel. Last summer our buddy Mike got his wedding ring caught in the die cutting machine and half his hand was gone before he knew it. That deep slow power that surrounds us unseen can snap shut any moment.

Sheila is waiting for me when I get home. I tell her we met the kids who found it. They were down in the gulch, fishing at the first spring thaw. They saw Jess's face through the window, the tangled cloud of her hair.

"Oh, Andrew." Sheila puts her hands over her heart. "The snow that night . . . remember I was watching the reports on TV, and I called you and told you to stay inside? She must have been off the road before she knew it." She comes over and gives me a hard hug, like it could have been me.

I will marry this girl, I will. As soon as I can accept that as I get older my choices get narrow and sharper, like knives.

I hold the casserole and a container of soup as we knock for a long time on Tom's door. When he answers, Sheila stretches one arm around him, her head not even reaching his shoulder.

"Oh, Tom, honey. I'm so sorry." She goes into the

kitchen and starts running water, banging around pots and pans. Women know what to say in these situations. They know what to do.

Tom sits on the couch and puts his hands over his face. The ring's back on his finger. He's wearing that awful, worn-out flannel shirt.

"You know what her last words to me were?"

He looks up and his eyes have the same expression our buddy Mike's did, not when it happened, but the days after.

"I love you. She had her hand on the door, and she was crying, and she looked back at me and said, 'I love you.'"

There's nothing I can say to that face. There are no words for this.

I let the dog out and stand on Tom's back porch, looking out at the woods and the fresh growth of trees.

When we were eight years old, a tornado tore through this town. It ripped mature oaks up by the roots, flattened barns and houses, threw cars into haystacks and people into electric wires.

To us kids the devastation was a playground, the ordinary all smashed and made new by a ramming fist of wind. But I remember that strange calm right before it hit: the sky empty and dark as a cave, everything paused and waiting, that immense pounding silence, and then the distant, high-pitched sucking of furious air.

It wouldn't have been fast. Like watching a ball head toward the net, a man's hand getting cut off, a shed being taken up board by board into the sky: time stretches in those instances, balloons and becomes infinitely slow. It would have taken a long, long time for the car to soar through the air, to hit and sink, to be covered over by snow. Long enough for her to think on everything.

Tom covers his face again. "I said, 'I love you too.' But she had already left."

Someday he'll ask me why Jess was headed to our house that night, when she knew Sheila was away. But now he's thinking of the obvious things: the way she looked when he first kissed her, her laugh when she was embarrassed, the white of her wedding dress.

I imagine her in the car all those months, calling out to me and to all of us, begging at last to be seen: pale skin still as glass, her eyes open and full of light, hair like seaweed floating up to the sky.

Saving Grace

Grace has discovered that she is shrinking.

She doesn't know exactly when it began but she can see the effects now when she studies herself in the mirror, which she was never in the habit of doing, even when she was fuller and there was more to her to look at. Something is slowly wearing her away, shaving off little layers of flesh and tissue with a sedate and murderous persistence.

As a child she used to study the illustrations under the entry for 'human' in her parents' encyclopedia. Dimly, through the overlay of glossy transparent pages, skin atop muscle and so on, she could see the colorful curving shapes of internal organs and behind that, the gleam of bone. She felt frightened for these people who had the softest and most tender parts of them exposed in graphic primary colors.

So it is with Grace. Her tendons stand out in bas-relief and her bones push at the underside of her skin. She can see the paths and highways of blood vessels through the few layers of epidermis that remain.

It disturbs her a little, this shape of her skeleton, the thrusting points of ribs and skull and spinal cord. It is indecent, this self-display. Soon other people will avert their eyes when she passes, embarrassed by her shamelessness. Cover thyself, woman, people will think at the sight of her arteries and muscles and bones, at the sight of her walking around with her insides showing.

She is becoming translucent. Soon one will be able to see light through her, like the sketch of a person on a glossy slide, like a smudge upon a chalkboard, the suggestion of a person who had once been there but had, without explanation, gone away.

*

GRACE IS MEEK at the doctor's office. She knows firsthand that there are very ill people in the world. She is aware of the cost of health insurance, that high-stakes gamble, that effort to ensure that your body doesn't get stolen from you like your furniture, your car stereo, your art.

The radio in the waiting room plays light rock. A woman croons about her broken heart.

Grace feels ridiculous sitting here on the blue couch, a young woman in a shabby spring jacket with a mud stain on the hem, the jacket she will throw away once all the snow has melted. She thinks about her own heart, her old heart, a heart made of tissues already worn out when it came to her. Her pants are too loose. Her sweater sags over the knobs of her shoulders.

The nurse crooks her arm around her clipboard and doesn't make eye contact. Grace submits to the measurements and the scale. The nurse reads out a number one and one-quarter inch shorter than the number Grace put on her driver's license when she moved to town.

How she can be shrinking? She shuffles down the carpeted hallways, carrying her shoes. She wants the poise, the presence of a tall woman, stature if not substance. She laments the passing of these inches. She wants her hair to sweep dramatically back from her face.

She follows the nurse to the brick of an examination room. She sits down on another blue couch. Stiff tissue-like paper crinkles beneath her. The nurse writes numbers in her folder, closes it, takes her pulse, opens the folder, looks at the numbers again. She looks at her watch. Her hand is warm and cool at the same time, a living hand but without affection. Grace wonders if she ought not hold her breath.

"You've lost fifteen pounds in the last six months," the nurse says. "Are you on a diet?"

"No," Grace says, and then wonders if she has lied. She wonders if losing your taste for certain foods should be confessed to your doctor. She wonders if it must be called a diet if you do not feel hungry much of the time.

In fourth grade she won the school-wide spelling bee on the word 'ravenous.' It is a word she understands the composition of, if not the sense.

"I am exercising," she volunteers.

She is a good patient. She schedules her check-ups when she is supposed to. She picks up her prescriptions on time and writes a check for her co-payment before she leaves. She is an uncomplaining cog in the great anonymous wheel of the industry of health provision.

Also, she walks to work each day.

"Your blood pressure is lower than last time, and so is your pulse."

The nurse folds up the arm cuff and replaces it on its hook. Grace pulls down the sleeve of her sweater, now stretched even more.

The nurse, she observes, is left-handed. After the fourth-grade spelling victory Grace went to the regional contest and lost on the word 'southpaw.' She spelled 'softball' instead. She was not a ball-player. Grace is right-handed. Whole worlds exist of which she is unaware.

"That word should not have been on the list," her mother said as they drove home, Grace with an ice cream sundae in her lap to console her. "Technically, it's slang."

"You're underweight," the nurse says. "You need

those fifteen pounds." She sounds accusing. Where did those fifteen pounds go? Where did you put them, Grace?

Grace remembers the silence that attended the defeat of each contestant, sometimes attended by the sigh of a watching parent. She might have been saved if she had asked that her word be used in a sentence.

When she made her appointment, she was asked to choose a physician. Grace floundered. She wanted to ask for a sweet grey-haired lady with gentle veined hands. Or a young woman whose parents moved to the U.S. because they dreamed their child would be a doctor. Grace likes to be around fulfilled dreams. Her own goals are insubstantial, hovering on the periphery of her vision, little sprites that disappear when looked at directly.

Finally, at random, Grace chose a name from the list and was embarrassed, at her first appointment, to discover that her new physician was young and male and good-looking. He had dark hair and a well-shaped face and, had she walked past him on the street, Grace would have turned to look. Now she sits on a plastic examining table with tissue paper wrapped around her chest and a nurse frowning in the corner.

"How are things today?" the doctor inquires, opening the folder and looking at it. Grace cannot tell if he is speaking to the nurse or to her.

"Weight loss," the nurse replies. "Lowered blood pressure, lower pulse."

On her inhale, Grace experiences that feeling of her heart getting stuck between two ribs. Something is caught and stabs her. It takes a few more breaths for the trapped part to work itself free. She is terrified that the doctor can sense this.

"Hmmm," the doctor murmurs.

Grace feels the nurse is on the lookout for

undeserved kindness. Probably most people weigh themselves occasionally. If their clothes become loose they check a scale; they do not assume that the clothing stores have altered their size measurements.

The nurse believes that Grace has been culpably ignorant. *Ignorant*, Grace spells in her head. Her mother spent hours drilling her for her regional performance. She prepared lists. She taught Grace etymology, word formation. *Culpa*, from the Latin, plus *able*, suffix. Her mother was excellent at inventing sentences. Grace is culpable of having a careless character.

"Hmmm." The doctor glances over the figures. "Have you been trying to lose weight?"

Grace studies her hands. Beneath the glaring fluorescent lamps of the exam room they appear bleached of all color, as white as bone. Perhaps that is bone, gleaming through the skin.

She feels lighter all over, curious about those missing inches, those vanished pounds. In the mirror above the sink she can measure the evaporation. Her hair, once a thick dark brown, now appears a wispy chestnut, lightening toward nondescript. Her eyes look more grey than green.

On the backs of her hands she can see her blood vessels like the delicate tracery of a highway map, rich dark red highways for arteries, purple country roads for veins. She tries hiding within her paper outfit but it just gaps open in new places, letting cool air rush across her skin.

The doctor hums to himself and warms the paddle of the stethoscope between his hands. Grace's heart shies like a colt. Easy, easy, she says to her own heart, convincing it to calm down, to trust her. She feels the painful burp of a ventricle, a solo blip, like a gurgle in the plumbing. She is still wearing her socks.

She looks at a corner of the ceiling while the dark head turns to her in profile and he listens to the racket inside her chest. Front, then back. Breathe in, now release. The paddle presses gently at all the usual points, as though he is putting something back in place.

Grace tries to imagine what he hears behind the slow and controlled breaths. She imagines it is a steady *lubb-dubb, lubb-dubb,* with a tiny drizzle behind it, like the drain on a bathtub not properly stoppered. Like a showoff, like a flirt, her heart gives its little giggle, a hiccup. Coyly it flutters over the missed beat, a child coming up flailing after a cartwheel.

Behave, Grace tells it sternly. Her heart is a toddler she can't take anywhere.

Her doctor frowns. The nurse frowns. Everyone is frowning. "You've been taking the beta blockers?" he asks.

Grace nods. At the university hospital, while she was still in school, the heart specialist told her to think of them as a vitamin. He explained their chemical function, but Grace still looks at the tiny green pill with the ß stamped on it and thinks, *vitamin.*

She takes it every morning after the birth control—her anti-pregnancy vitamin—and before the horse pill of the multivitamin, loaded with zinc and copper and fiberglass and all those other strange minerals that should be in road cement, in the windows of buildings, but not in human flesh.

She imagines the ß the autograph of its superpowers, the seat of the beta rays it sends out to reinforce the walls and valves of her heart. *Zap! Pow!* Look at this heart, strong and steady and magnificent.

She thinks of her heart as something she has been given custody of, a problem child, a medical case. She can pull it out and show its picture, rendered in full color on special glossy pages, just like the pictures in the encyclopedia. Her very own Greek alchemist, the heart specialist. This beta-rayed heart shall never fail.

"I'm going to order an EKG," the doctor says. "We want to be certain."

Of what? Grace wants to ask, but does not. The doctor and nurse depart, leaving Grace to stew over acronyms. Why not ECG? Is it not, after all, an electro-cardiogram?

She had to have one before, back in the days of the heart specialist. She cannot recall if it hurt. Many parts of her hurt back in those days.

The nurse returns pushing a computer printer on a chest-high cart. It is not a state-of-the-art printer, not laser, not even inkjet; at most, a dot-matrix. Several paddles are attached. They resemble the battery cables Grace bought and stored in the trunk of her new car, months ago, when she moved to her new apartment in the new city where she had gotten a new job.

Grace is instructed to lie down. The paper vest is removed briefly, baring acres of white flesh. Grace imagines herself a marble statue. She imagines herself a vase like that holding the bouquet of sunflowers in the print taped to the ceiling.

"This won't hurt," the nurse says and attaches several small stickers to Grace's chest and then her ankles, pushing down her socks. Indeed the stickers do not hurt at all. Also, they do not stick to Grace's skin. The nurse pokes through a drawer in search of tape.

Grace feels very fragile as she lies there attached to a machine sketching the beat of her heart. She cannot see the printout. She does not want to turn her head and upset anything. She might put a dangerous jagged edge where no valley or mountain belongs.

She feels the nurse can sense that at home, at her new adult apartment, Grace has a little girl's bedroom.

That she has a pyramid of Elinor's stuffed animals in the corner. It would be impossible to explain to anyone why she has all of her little sister's stuffed animals, even the newer ones with which Elinor never played.

Also it would be difficult to explain why she carefully transported the menagerie from her little sister's bedroom, taking careful notes of the placement of each animal, of the precise angulations of trunk and paw and ear which allowed the delicate pyramid to support itself. Probably the nurse's daughter has her own collection of stuffed animals, but the daughter is likely much younger than Grace.

She is not given the EKG printouts for inspection. No one expects her to know what it means. She is only the keeper, the body, the chamber in which this curious heart is stored. It is given to other people to explore, to explain it, to study its mechanics. It is at their discretion to explain anything to her.

The nurse says, "You may dress now," and slips soundlessly out the door, and as Grace lifts an arm to put into the sleeve of her sweater, her heart gives a gulp that makes her left arm tingle for a moment. This is a trick it is still rehearsing, that it does when no one is looking. Grace is grateful that it waited.

A LEAKY VALVE, the heart specialist explained, is like slippage. Not all the blood gets through that should, so your heart works harder than normal.

Grace nodded. All through her school years she worked harder than normal. She was Grace the super pupil, Grace the star. Grace Atkins, valedictorian. Grace Atkins, *summa cum laude*. She made her mother proud. Grace reasoned that if her heart was working harder, the blood cells were pumping through her at a faster rate than normal. There was more life in every square inch of her. That was her, Grace Atkins, over-achiever.

A heart murmur of grade one is the lowest, the heart specialist said. That means you miss anywhere up to one in every six beats. Grace nodded again. It was difficult to be attentive when she was sitting in bed wearing a robe that had no fastenings except a button at the neck and a tie in the middle of her back.

It was too big—there was more air than her in it, and at some point it had occurred to Grace that sick people had worn this robe, that all manner of bodily fluids had been leaked or spilled or spattered on this robe during its lifetime. She tried not to let it touch her skin in too many places.

Her rear hurt from shivering in hospital beds for a day and a half. Apparently it was the rule in hospitals to keep the air at a temperature at which bacterial life could not survive. She wanted a pair of flannel pajamas and the bliss of being in her own bed, decently clothed. She did not want to discuss statistics.

One in six was a very poor batting average. But excellent odds for the lottery. Grace sat in the room that night watching black-and-white cartoons with the lights off and held a hand to her chest, feeling the beat of her heart.

Most times it ticked on as regular as a clock, but at moments it paused altogether, gathering itself for a couple of spastic beats, the fluttering of bird's wings beneath her rib cage. An assembly worker, day-dreaming for a moment and forgetting to keep her hand on the button that moved the conveyor belt along, then hurrying to correct her error when she realized things were beginning to back up behind her. She could run at full speed for a couple moments and cover her mistake, for the time being. But those daydreaming workers were unreliable, couldn't be trusted. One day they might just drop everything and walk off the job. Leave completely.

Later, Grace did the reading on mitral valve prolapse—Grace was a super student, she always did the reading—and it fascinated her that pig heart valves were sometimes used to replace the human ones. Imagine! She couldn't quite see how it could all work together, that alien bit of tissue attached to the human fabric. Those were pig cells. What if they were ungovernable by the human brain?

Just let her cerebellum try to exercise any authority over some stubborn, wayward pig tissue. Pig valve! the cerebellum would say. Pump! You know your cue! And there the pig valve would be, off doing its own thing, rooting disobediently in a corner. It might pump madly for a time or refuse to work altogether. The blood would back up behind it, cells milling about and platelets crowding, bloated with the oxygen they were supposed to ferry to the rest of the body. What would happen then? Would the heart just explode?

Poor heart, Grace thought. It was not slipping because it was working harder. It slipped because it was weary of the endless demand upon it to pump, pump, pump, not a moment's rest, not a second. Bear this grief, that disappointment, this growing list of failures. It gave up a little more with each added weight. Her blood plodded through her arteries with diminishing enthusiasm. One after another the cells would go AWOL until she disintegrated into a tracery of herself, printed on cardboard, then tissue paper, and then—she supposed eventually she would come to this—nothing but light and air.

THE FIFTEEN POUNDS perplex her as she sits in bed that night. In the corner, on a trunk that holds several sets of clothes which first belonged to Grace and then to Elinor and now again to Grace, Elinor's tower of stuffed animals rises in a babble of color. The pyramid is not doing so well. It requires the support of the wall.

Grace has irrational thoughts while the fingers of her masseuse rub circles across her back. The masseuse is Eric, who lives across the hall.

Grace wonders where weight goes when it disappears. Does it convert to energy? Perhaps the energy is floating around, trapped behind the dresser, stuck in the closet every time she shuts the door.

It is rather like wondering where spirits go when the body dies. She is afraid the same principles of energy conservation might apply. If so then it is entirely possible that Elinor is trapped somewhere beneath that pile of stuffed animals and she, Grace, is responsible.

"You're tiny," Eric says in an echo of her current concern. He curves his fingers over her shoulder and traces the cliff of her collarbone with his fingertips.

"I'm not that much shorter than you," Grace answers.

Eric can beat her at anything to do with math but depends on her to correct his hopeless spelling. Tall and lanky, with wide shoulders and chipped teeth—the body of a pole vaulter, the body of a pole—Eric sees the world in numerical expressions. He is a mathematician and a philosopher.

Grace likes his hands, long-fingered and slender. When she stands next to him he feels solid as a wall, strong enough for her to lean on. When they hug, her nose comes to the top of his shoulder. Eric likes to stand behind her and wrap his arms around her and him, which his arms are long enough to do. Grace feels like a larva in a cocoon, encased and immobile, a position she is not entirely sure she likes.

Eric strokes his hands over her back, over her

pajama top. "I can feel every one of your ribs."

"I'll bet I could feel yours if I tried," Grace retaliates.

Eric has lit candles. He is playing a CD of operatic love songs, something he dug out of her collection, something she bought eons ago when she still believed in opera. She is not sure she is ready for him to know this about her.

Eric's hands on her skin press warmly like the paddle of the stethoscope, gently, like the doctor's hands. Grace's heart limps along. In the stillness she can sense the pain as sound. One in seven. One in five.

Eric wraps his fingers around her wrists, measuring the thinness of her bones. "You're like a bird," he says. "Look at this. I can fit both my hands around your waist." His fingertips and thumbs overlap.

"What kind of bird?" Grace asks him. She does not like feeling little and helpless, able to be snapped.

Little creatures are ridiculous when they try to be fearsome, like tiny dogs shrilling at strangers, shadows, newspapers blowing in the wind. Big things are taken seriously. A tiger for instance did not have to attempt to appear fearsome; tigers can walk, lie down, sleep wherever they want to. No one ever nags tigers about their weight.

"Are you being facetious?" Eric wants to know.

Grace remembers being surprised when she learned 'facetious' was spelled with an F instead of a V. Her father used the word often. Eric used it in their first conversation.

She recognized him at the bagel shop where she stopped each day for breakfast. The way he moved his arms attracted her, how he threw hot bagels into the top baskets, his forearms flexing as he cut cheese. He used his hands to add another dimension to speech.

The first time she ordered bagels for the office, he

paused to explain the research he was doing for his dissertation, something that involved fearsomely complicated equations. Grace clutched the paper bag to her stomach and looked at the way his hair stuck out from under his cap and the way his lower teeth leaned against one another, and she knew at some point he would ask to be with her and she knew she would say yes.

"Tonight?" Eric whispers against her neck. "Are you in the mood tonight?"

The tiny hairs at her nape lift up and then lie back down. She and Eric are almost the same age. The amount of time he had spent in graduate school, Grace spent at a cancer research center, in a special ward reserved for pediatric derivations of the disease.

She was not a patient. She was there for moral support. Not life support, as it turned out; she had not been able to provide that.

In her reading she had discovered that 'vulnerable' was not *vuler* plus *nable* as she had supposed. Vulnerable, from the Latin *vulnerare*, to wound.

An organism with a seriously suppressed immune system is particularly vulnerable to ailments. When two people are in a relationship they are vulnerable. Each has the power to wound.

Grace contemplates the lingering pressure around her waist and wrists. "How about we hold each other," she whispers.

Candlelight flickers in the curious jet eyes of the stuffed animals in the corner. All of her carnal appetites have been fading. Desire can no longer penetrate her skin. She is becoming more porous; these things blow right through her.

She lies down, pulling him beside her. On the stereo the tenor softly croons. She can feel the vibrations inside her chest, and inside of Eric's when she puts her arms around him, one of her knees between his.

He is comfortably solid, substantial. She hopes that if a big wind comes he will anchor her. She hopes that if he were to see her dry out and shrivel up, he would reach out and cup her gently and not allow her to blow away.

A FEW DAYS later, Grace drives two hours north to visit her parents for their weekly dinner, leaving behind the city in its bed of lakes and following the hills of farmland to her childhood home. She decides not to mention her doctor's appointment.

Her mother greets her holding one of those plastic cups that come free with the combination meal. It is filled with vodka. She does not offer to mix a cocktail for Grace.

Her father looks at television, not watching, just staring. The light from the screen flashes over his face but the images never penetrate the skin.

For dinner they turn off the television and light candles and use the good china. Grace's mother opens a bottle of wine for Grace and her father and adds cocktail onions to her second vodka tonic, happy that she is not drinking alone. To Grace's mother only alcoholics drink alone, and they get drunk on hard liquor, scotch or whiskey, or simply drink too much beer as Grace's grandfather used to do.

Grace does not look at her mother and see in her the little girl who locked herself in her room so the blows fell on the door instead of on skin. She believes it is rude to pry into certain things. It is rude to ask someone to expose their insides. It is almost criminal.

Grace reports on the concert she attended with Eric. She affirms that she still likes her job and is often invited to lunch by her co-workers. She enjoys her apartment but has not yet used her membership at the gym. There is sadly little news of note that has transpired during the week. Grace feels slightly guilty for this.

Grace's mother does not ask her if she stopped by the cemetery; she knows Grace has. She will see the handful of daisies when she makes her own pilgrimage later in the week to water the rose bushes. Grace imagines the cemetery calls to her mother the same way it calls to her, with the cool quiet graves, the utter stillness of the organized rows, the clarity of carved dates.

A few feet away from Elinor is the tiny grave where her grandmother years ago buried a baby, a little girl who did not live a year. A needle jabs Grace's heart every time she sees a new basket of flowers at this grave. Her mother, too, has lost a sister. This should bring them closer. It should be something they can talk about as they sit in silence in the living room. Grace suspects that her mother thinks all too often of that graveyard as she sits in her armchair with her martini glass, stares out the window examining her life and wondering how it has come, exactly, to this.

They are careful with one another. They talk around sharp edges. They refrain from saying words that could sound accusatory. They do not speak of anniversaries or of looming birthdays or of absent family members.

They do not conduct themselves as though they have been injured. They avert their eyes the way Grace would avoid looking at an amputee's missing limb or the scars of a failed suicide; there is a certain decorum that must be maintained among survivors.

In the middle of the black-and-white movie Grace's mother turns to her. "Why don't we come down and take you to dinner next Friday."

Grace's father looks around in surprise.

"If you don't mind the drive," Grace says. "You could stay in my spare room."

"We wouldn't want to put you to any trouble," her mother says at the next commercial break, stirring her freshened martini.

"It wouldn't be any trouble," says Grace.

Silence falls in the dim room. In the middle of a car chase her mother says, "We could meet Eric. He could come to dinner with us."

"I'm sure he'd like that," Grace says. "I'll ask him."

In her chest her heart scrabbles at her like a clawed thing. She wonders if Eric will want to meet her parents. She wonders if Eric has begun to concern himself about the future. He might be making actuary computations about whether she is a bad risk. He might be thinking, As a girlfriend, Grace makes a great proofreader.

"Don't go to any trouble," her mother says. "We wouldn't want that."

SUNDAY GRACE GOES to the convenience store and buys hair color. She buys self-tanning ointment that promises to give her skin a healthy bronze glow. Then she goes to the ladies apparel store to visit the burgundy suit she has been thinking of buying. It will clash fashionably with her new auburn hair.

She tries on the outfit in her usual size and is astonished to find that it hangs off her. She lends no more shape to this suit than the clothes hanger.

"Can I help you with anything?" the salesgirl calls over the fitting-room door.

"I need a smaller size," says a humiliated Grace.

"Oh, that looks so nice on you," the salesgirl says with forced enthusiasm once Grace slides into the smallest size they have. She glares at Grace with envy.

Grace does not think the salesgirl would want her figure if she knew the price tag attached to it. She would be happy with her vital, seamless, outrageous heart.

At the nail salon Grace sits through an hour-long manicure. She watches music videos while the nail technician applies three separate coats of coffee brown polish to her nails with delicate precision. The technician's small daughter plays with a stuffed blue elephant in the chair reserved for those getting an eyebrow wax. She smiles at Grace and strokes the elephant's velvety blue ears.

Grace smiles back. Despite trying to be careful she scratches her thumbnail when she opens the door to leave, making a deep neat incision into the layers of matte polish, exposing the pearly pink beneath.

She is walking down the street back to her car when she sees them, the man and the woman in front of the secondhand clothing store.

The man, perhaps mid-thirties, has a thick cap of jet black hair. He stands close to the woman as though guarding her while she examines the antique dresses.

Her loose clothing and her stance are a clear and familiar beacon to Grace. Her shoulders bow slightly inward, drawn with the gravity of a persistent pain. She has decided not to wear a hat or bandana or wig, and instead a colorful scarf wraps her naked head.

Grace respects this choice: tasteful, and the most comfortable option. She remembers wheeling Elinor down the hospital hall to the wig room and laughing at the ridiculous choices, bouffant Dolly Parton or sleek Jackie Kennedy, nothing that could replace the wild honey mop of a twelve-year-old girl.

She remembers the stares when she brought Elinor to the mall one afternoon, a rare afternoon away from the hospital. The clothing stores did not space their clothing racks far enough apart to accommodate a wheelchair. In defiance Grace plucked item after item from the rack and paraded them before Elinor, draping her with rayon, with stretch nylon, with 100% cotton and raw silk.

None of the salesgirls invited Elinor to try something on. In the end they bought nothing and Grace left the discarded clothing in a heap beneath a display of linen shirts, like an outlaw ditching her booty. She took Elinor to the food court and they ate Cinnabons and salted pretzels and then went to see a movie and ate gummi bears and popcorn and sour drops and nearly everybody tripped over Elinor's wheelchair because it stuck out into the row.

Grace feels a bond with this jealous man. She and he understand the things you try to do because of the things you cannot do, for instance restore someone's thinning blood cells, take the toxins into one's own body, return an identity that has become tangled with the diagnosis of a disease. She imagines he would open his own chest and take out his heart, bleeding in offering. Take it, will you? If it cannot heal you what use is it to me?

Of course that was before they learned about her own heart, her porous heart, her pervious heart, which limps madly along at a full gallop. *Lubb-a-dubb-dubb* is the chant of her heart, then a moment of silence.

Grace looks down at the sidewalk as she walks toward the couple, believing she is respectful by not staring. She has seen how a body can waste away and turn itself into nothingness. It does not surprise her to think that her own fading might be no more than a sympathetic echo. The gap inside her began as a dark hole in her heart and instead of closing it is spreading. One day there will be more of the nothingness that was once Grace than there ever has been of Grace.

She imagines emitting beta rays as she passes. The rays reach out to enfold all three of them and nothing can ever harm them again.

ON THURSDAY Grace wears her new burgundy suit. It is Elinor's birthday. It is also the day of her six-month review.

Her department manager and supervisor take Grace out to lunch to celebrate the completion of her probationary period. The outdoor market, in a glorious fit of optimism, has opened for business. Grace stops to examine the sunflowers rioting on a corner. She imagines them blossoming madly in someone's greenhouse all during the dark winter. She buys two bunches, one for home, one for the office. Her manager is surprised. It seems no one has bought flowers for the office before.

This is the first real conversation Grace has had with her department manager. She imagines he did not want to get too friendly in case she didn't work out. She imagines one only invests in the permanent employees.

Grace dreads these conversations, the basic descriptions of domicile and background, education and family, like taking the blood pressure or pulse. These questions are never unthreatening. Her hometown: mid-sized city, mid-sized high school, middle-class in every respect. Her education, the usual four-year-degree, with a gap she does not feel she needs to address. Pleasant and not too large circle of friends. Parents, two. Siblings?

The sun burns Grace's small segment of sidewalk, shining like the torch of the inquisitor. Grace moved to town keeping Elinor a secret. It was nobody's wound but her own. It was also not a way to open conversations. She does not know how to answer this.

To say nothing is to renounce Elinor, to deny and betray her, to sweep aside her existence in an unthinkable act of dismissal. So she says simply, "A sister," and around the sunflowers she feels a pulse in her palms. One out of six beats. One out of six. Very regular today.

Her supervisor is being extra friendly. She sees Grace has been a hit with the department manager and wants to make her own approval clear. "Oh, how old?" she inquires with a wide, lethal smile.

Grace feels the silk shirt sticking to her skin. There is an Elinor she carries inside her head and this Elinor has currently expanded to fill her vision. It is just like the spelling bee when all she could see was an enormous softball in her head and she heard the dissected words, silly letters, issuing from her mouth. Here they are again, the little betrayals, while her heart does cartwheels, launching itself again and again against her ribs, as though trying to get itself stuck.

"She'd be thirteen today," Grace says. "But she died eleven months ago." Eleven months, fourteen days, two hours and forty seconds. Forty-one. Forty-two. Forty-three.

Grace feels it in the chalky air: something has been released. The tilt of the sun reveals the shadow behind her. She is still the new editorial assistant, a competent and likeable person, in dress-code-conforming attire and skillful makeup, bright hair, fingernail polish in a suitable shade. But now they can see how her edges have become milky and blurred by darkness.

Inside her ribcage her heart knocks itself out for a moment and lies there gasping. She tightens her hands around the furry stems and feels sticky paste in the crevices of her palms.

"I'm sorry," her manager says, and her supervisor

nods her condolences.

"Thank you," Grace says.

She once used to say, bitterly, I'm sorry, too. Sorry to lose her sister, her bright-eyed Elinor, brave Elinor, naughty Elinor, bewildered, sick, and no-longer-laughing Elinor, with her thick blonde curls and strong firm body cannibalized by itself. Now after eleven months Grace understands that "I'm sorry" is no more than an admission, an acknowledgement, a silent salute of helplessness. A promise to be careful, or at least try.

THAT AFTERNOON, on Elinor's birthday, her doctor calls.

"The EKG appears normal," he says, "but I want to take another look at your heart."

Grace fusses with the sunflowers on her kitchen table, trying to prop up their drooping heads.

"I want to run some more tests," he says.

Her parents are coming the next day. Grace vacuums the floor and puts fresh sheets on the spare bed. She clears the expired dairy products from her refrigerator. Then she goes into her bedroom.

The Babel tower of stuffed animals regards her trustfully. Their fates are in her hands. They can only hope she will show mercy.

Grace presses a hand to her chest and wonders what the doctor could be concerned about. The beat is firm and regular. The tiny little flutter revealed through the stethoscope is undetectable to the naked ear.

It's her own secret, this flaw deep inside her chest cavity, her heart slowly wearing down. She imagines the blood cells in her body, dizzy with oxygen, spinning along their assigned network of arteries and capillaries. *Whee!* When the flow pauses she imagines they stop and look at each other like people on a malfunctioning amusement park ride, first surprised and then a little panicked, questioning each other. What's going on?

"Am I keeping you here?" Grace asks the stuffed animals. "Have I trapped you all this time?"

They look back at her with glassy jet eyes. Grace strokes their velour hair, their stuffed polyester bodies and giddy shirts. And then, mane and paw, she begins to dismantle the pyramid.

"YOU'VE CLEANED everything," Eric says in surprise when he comes over later that night. "You're even cleaning your closet?"

He enters the bedroom carrying the plastic carryout bag of food, wafting the scent of soy sauce and shrimp fried rice everywhere. He picks up the one grayish stuffed lump that stands in the place of the pyramid. "What is this?"

"That's Fantine," Grace says. "I'm keeping her."

The rest of the animals nestle contentedly in a garbage bag in the corner, all except the elephant, now washed clean of Elinor's two-year-old baby drool, once her favorite toy and now Grace's sacred charge.

The animals do not seem upset. Grace will offer them to her parents first, and if they decline she will take the bag to the hospital. She will deliver it to the children's ward.

She will not purposefully look for the woman in the scarf, but if she sees her, it would not be unreasonable to say hello. It would not be unreasonable to ask her about antique dresses.

"My parents are coming to visit tomorrow," she says. "They want to know if you'd like to go to dinner with us."

"Is that what the sunflowers are for?" Eric says.

Sunflowers. Grace loved the simple words that became something mysterious, something more, when put in a compound. Something magical. A flower that held the sun. She could tell him that for years Elinor planted sunflowers in their mother's garden, and every year the birds ate the seeds before Elinor could.

She would like to tell him the sunflowers remind her of the light the afternoon her sister's doctor said there was nothing left they could do for her. Elinor was sleeping; her last lucid moment had come and gone. The sunset that evening was the most beautiful Grace had ever seen. The color bronzed her father's face as he reached across the bed to take her mother's hand.

Grace held Elinor's hand between both of hers. She watched the sunflowers on the windowsill droop and shed their petals because she had forgotten to put water in the vase. She didn't rise to correct this. She felt her own pulse fall into rhythm with Elinor's, beating in tandem, in companionship, until late, late that night, in the abandoned hour between one day and the next, that pulse slowed, and slowed, and then stopped. Grace felt that silence through every inch of her, like a reed in the wind, pure and clear.

"The sunflowers," she says, "are for my sister."

Eric looks at her wonderingly. "You never told me you have a sister," he says. "Where is she?"

Grace herself would like an answer to that question. In a pile before her tumble the things that belonged to but were not Elinor herself, are only the leavings, the sediment, a name on the stone of a grave.

Nobody ever spelled Elinor's name right. They wanted her to be Eleanor like the First Lady, or Ellen, or Nora, or some such. E-L-I-N-O-R, Grace at last began to introduce her. From Helen, from the Greek, which means light.

This time she permits the hard words, she lays them before him like a gift.

"She had leukemia," Grace says. For the second time her heart, in a passing moment, stuns itself. She wonders if this ever becomes easier. She does not imagine that it does.

Gently Eric touches the stacks of clothing, the items that Grace has pulled out of the box. He smells like the afternoon shift at the bagel shop. He touches the fabric like it might still contain heat, the detritus of a supernova, the remains of a bright and very lovely star.

"What I want to know," Grace says, "is if you would like to have dinner with my parents."

He moves close, wrapping both arms around them. He is tangible, solid. Grace listens to the cadence of his heartbeat, strong and slow. Her blood cells wash through the pathways beneath her skin, ripples spreading over a quiet lake.

She remembers a family vacation to the seaside when Elinor was four. The waves knocked her down again and again, and thinking she was drowning they ran to where she lay shrieking and splashing in the surf to find Elinor laughing, eyes tearing, lips stinging with salt. Grace wonders how she could ever let go of this, let this tide move away from her and come back eventually, stretching its fingers back to land but never in the same place, always returning but never as it once was, not lost but changed, and changing still.

Care of the Soul

So you know how sometimes you get this announcement from the universe on who you are and what you're supposed to be doing, and it's so loud and clear and "this is what I mean" that you really can't afford to ignore it?

Okay, so maybe not everyone. But I was taking my walk around the pond today and I got one of these hello check-ins. I saw these two other ladies I haven't seen before, and they had these walking sticks, and I figured the tall one, with white hair, was maybe training for a long mountain trek, but the wide, short one was leaning on these flimsy little aluminum things like she was just out of rehab. I would have said they were both older than me, but you never can tell with the things that will wear on a woman.

They were headed clockwise and I was going widdershins, so I crossed them at the scarlet oak tree— it's an arboretum, so all the special plants have little signs with their names on them. The wide one had an out-of-a-bottle dye job and I wanted to tell her look, honey, if you're going to fight it, pay for a salon. Those might have been tears on her eyes or just the sun in her glasses, but she looked up at her friend with this wide-eyed, protesting, exasperated expression and said, "Look, you know, sometimes you just need a little time for your*self!*"

I nodded as I passed, feeling soft and big-hearted toward the both of them. On another day I'd have walked up to them, said hi, my name is Stella—it means Star, it belonged to a great-aunt but it belongs more to me, and I could have been one, I think, a star, or at least famous for something, if my mama had gotten me a talent agent when I was four, if I'd ever figured out what I'm good at. Time was I would have asked them about their kids, because they both probably had kids of some sort.

I wouldn't have asked about their jobs because they were both either retired or never had one, not to speak of—I know the type. I could have asked them if they were in some occupational therapy program, I know lots about therapy, or if they were fixing to go on a hiking trip, just the two of them, a friend's getaway. I would have approved. But I didn't approach them, not today, because sister had it right, what she said. Sometimes you just need a little time for yourself.

I have lots of that these days, and I earned it. Which isn't to say I don't enjoy people. There are lots of people in my building, mostly transients who are coming and going, some who have been there a while and might be there a long time to come.

I can tell you how it goes. Don't buy anything from Ernie because it's probably stolen. You go to him to replace a wallet or a phone that you think you lost, and there he is, trying to sell your own wallet back to you. Henry is all right when he's on his meds—that's true of many people, I guess—but don't catch him when the doctor is tinkering with his dose, he gets meaner than a skunk eating bumblebees.

Franz has got it rougher than anyone because he's black, so while people round here might look at a guy like Ernie and think he's just had a couple of bad shakes, they look at Franz and think he's a criminal, even though he is the sweetest, gentlest man you will ever meet. He's the one who saves part of his lunch from the soup kitchen and then takes it outside to feed the mangy dogs snuffling around the dumpster.

There aren't many women in the crowd; I guess I'm it for the full-timers. Most of the women coming through have a herd of kids and get put in the family shelter where they have their own laundry and bathrooms and a game room and they don't have to mingle with those of us *sans* house.

Though I'm not really a full-timer because I don't have a room for the long-term. I prefer to pack up each day and carry my stuff in the backpack, never make plans for the night, because you never know what will come up—a better job, a winning lottery ticket, an itching to see Sarasota.

I ain't one of those crazy ladies you see in the movies with all their sweaters piled on their back pushing a grocery cart of cans and toilet paper. I don't think those people actually exist, not even in Los Angeles, because really, all those cans? They're noisy and they're easy to steal.

I wash my clothes every night in the sink in my room and damp cotton will dry pretty fast on the skin or in a room that's decently heated. I can go to Elly's on the square and get a coffee and toast for $2.00. Sometimes I admit I spend it on a Krispy Kreme when I'm crossing town to work and the light goes on.

The library opens at ten. Before then you can go to the video store and pretend you're looking at the latest release; after that you can go to the half-price bookstore, the owner there is usually good about letting people wander or even read, if you can stand him bitching about the city council with his cronies.

If you don't have any cash that day the soup kitchen serves at six, and the rooms, if there's one available, open at eight. I've been getting room ten a lot lately. I like the round, solid shape of that number—10—but I'm not getting cozy. It's not a home. I don't need a home; that's my point.

There's a nice preacher lady who comes on Saturdays and sits in the common room and invites you to sit and chat. She's from the Episcopalian church or some such so there's no hellfire or castigating you for your sins, she just wants to hear your story, and I suppose she can give you a blessing or absolution if you're in need of either.

She asks me to tell her about my husband, my kids, but I'd rather tell her stories about my time down south because I would just love to make her eyes pop. She's been on missions I guess in Costa Rica, Guatemala, Ecuador, the like, so she's seen most of what I'm telling her already. It makes a better story with the guys.

I don't talk about my husband because he's not my husband anymore. He hung up that hat when he went stepping out with a mistress and I will tell you one thing, you get a free pass for a long time to do whatever you want when your husband cheats on you. You can gain all the weight or finally lose it, you can dye your hair or cut it, you can turn into a melted puddle of pity or you can whoop it up and drop everything and head south to Brazil, and all your friends will say good for her, he left her and the kids are grown and this is her time now, to figure out what she wants to do.

Of course the kids weren't really grown, they were still in high school, but they didn't seem to need me and he said if he got custody, he'd pay off the credit card debt. I could start fresh. So I cut my hair, cut up the credit cards, shed forty pounds and the bad ankles, and went to Rio de Janeiro. All I'll say about it is that I learned a lot about the world. Sometimes there is more cash and sometimes there is less cash, and you learn to land on your feet.

The counselor who comes to talk to us says I'm a good candidate for housing, I could probably get assistance of some sort, but once you get on a program like that they lock you down with all sorts of rules. I'm a good candidate because I have a job, not a job that pays enough for rent on an apartment, but enough for food and the city bus and occasional phone calls or clothes from the Goodwill, and the workers at the Dollar General are good about letting you know when they're rotating stock and a bunch of food is about to get thrown out.

Granola bars, applesauce, chips of every variety will last you on the days the soup kitchen's not serving. Those little kids Lunchables can go a long way and all that happens when the meat is old is that it gets very sweet, like candy, and it only upsets the tummy for a minute or two. Soup doesn't need to be warmed up though there's a microwave in the common room that you can use for free, you just have to try your luck that there are any plastic spoons available. I bring my own.

My job is that I drive a bus, the school bus, and there's nothing I love more. I passed the background check since nothing about Brazil showed up on my record and I'm a good employee. I'm careful with the equipment, I'm good with the kids, and I don't miss days because I'm not on meds or an addict and I'm not sick. I thank my lucky stars every day that they put me on Katie's route.

It's been such a pleasure watching that girl grow up. We started out purely by accident. I got the job the year she started kindergarten, and when there were problems with some other people who kept calling in sick or not showing, I got moved to Katie's route.

There she was with her Dora the Explorer backpack and her big solemn brown eyes and her hair that her mama can't do anything with, too thin and fine to hold a clip or a ponytail and she never will wear a headband. So it just hangs loose and sometimes gets into her eyes and she squints up at me with the sweetest little look and says every day, as she hikes up the big step, "Good morning, Miss Stella."

Every time she says my name I want to lean back and yell it like Marlon Brando does on that movie where he's lounging around with all his hunky muscles in that thin T-shirt and he keeps bellowing at his wife, not the sulky Scarlett O'Hara lady but that other one. I seem to pass that movie playing all the time in stores or restaurants and I always want to laugh, hearing Brando yelling my name. "Stellll-la!"

Like I mean something. Like I'm important. Like I feel when Katie says my name, greets me directly, 'cause not all the kids do, so many of them, even the bigger ones, just look right past you as they come up the stair, eager to find their friends and sit and chatter and you're just the mechanism who opens the door and then shuts it.

But Katie never forgets, every time she steps on I get a good morning, every time she steps down I get a "bye." I'm proud of her and proud that her mama taught her to be polite to strangers.

I've never seen Audrey at the bus stop, not to see her daughter off and not to collect her at the end of the day, it's always some neighbor lady retrieving a group of kids, so I imagine Audrey is working. Always so serious, that's where Katie gets it from.

I assume she's still married. I don't know. I could ask Mike but he only e-mails me two or three times a year—which is about as often as I check my e-mail— and then it's to tell me about his new job, his new girlfriend, the city he's living in or just left. It's almost like he's following in my footsteps, except I know he makes enough to pay rent.

So I was thinking about these ladies and their conversation when I went to the library, because it was a no-school day, Labor Day or one of those, and the guys wanted me to get that documentary about penguins waddling around the Arctic that had been popular a few years back and now suddenly, in some weird stroke of groupthink, they all wanted to watch.

And I was walking down the sidewalk in the sun thinking about that wide lady with her glasses and how much better I felt every day after I'd shed those forty pounds, like my ankles had been given new life, and there she was, dancing down the street, with Dora the Explorer strapped on her back and a headband shoved helter-skelter into her hair and a cute little dress with purple and white stripes.

I don't know why it is but there's nothing that lifts the spirits more than seeing a happy little kid going about her business of enjoying life, and at that age— she's six now, in first grade, so grown up and independent—they're just about perfect, old enough to look like real little people but not old enough to have acne or braces or trying to be popular and cool. She was just dancing along, singing to herself, lighting up the whole world, and then she paused, slowed down, stopped, looked up at me, and said, with her solemn little stare and her bangs falling into her eyes, "Well, hello, Miss Stella. You're not on the bus."

"And neither are you," I said. "Hello, Katie."

And then, because there was no way to avoid it, I looked at her mother.

She stood dead still and stared at me, though I hate to say it, with her mouth hanging open. She always could have been a pretty girl if she'd just tried.

Her brown hair was very short, almost butch, and those awful freckles were still all over her face, but she'd kept herself thin, or close to it, and she was dressed nicely, slacks and a button-down shirt. She had her cell phone to her ear—I was sorry to see she was one of those mothers, not going to remember these years with her kid—but then I don't remember much about when she was six, only that I would heave myself every day through the housework so that I could drop onto the couch with my soaps and a can of soda, and then plow through dinner and homework and baths so I could finally drop into bed and hope everything would stop aching. She was sixteen when her father cheated and most of those years between are a blur, even worse than Rio.

"Hello, Audrey," I said.

She still had her phone to her ear. "I don't effing believe this," she said.

"Language," I said, at the same time Katie said, "Mama, that's a swear."

When the glare turned to her daughter, I jumped in. "I'm back."

"I guess you are." She clipped the phone to her purse with a furious scowl. "It would have been nice to know that."

I answered without thinking. It's a fault of mine. "Why?"

"Why?" Her voice rose. "Why?"

Katie stood on the sidewalk, looking back and forth between us, edging toward her mother's knees. "I have a son now, did you know that? He's two."

Good for her, I thought, she lost the baby weight. Maybe that was why I never saw her at the corner, busy with the boy.

"I don't suppose you want to see your grandchildren. Want to see them grow up."

"I see her every day, Mama," Katie said. "She drives my bus."

"She drives," Audrey said, "your bus."

It was very hard talking to her like this, with her eyes behind the sunglasses. People forget that it's rude.

I shrugged again, turning my hands up. I do it a lot.

It's something little kids do, as a defense, that helpless, don't-beat-up-on-me pose. That I-have-no-idea-what-I'm-doing-here expression.

"I was lucky," I said. "I got your route."

"Lucky," she said. "Unbelievable." She put her hand on Katie's shoulder, fingers and thumbs pressing in, so she could steer her or yank her away. "So you have a job, at least. You're in the country. Where are you living? Does Dad know you're in town? Does Mike?"

"Yeah," I said. "They know. I think."

I couldn't remember. I don't tell Mike much, just that I enjoy his e-mails and keep writing. I don't talk to her father. At all.

"So I'm the only one who didn't know," she said. "Jesus Christ."

"You really shouldn't take the Lord's name in vain," I said. At the same time, Katie said, "Mama."

"I figured I'd get myself together first," I said. "You know, get established." I was doing it, that's hands-up, don't-shoot-I'm-innocent posture. "Then I was going to look you up. I'd love to see the little guy."

She sneered at me. My own daughter. As if I'm a coward or something.

"Of course you were," Audrey said. She pulled her purse across her chest like she was protecting herself from a bullet. "You were going to look us up."

"There, now," I heard myself saying, exactly as if she were back to being a colicky baby and I was trying to rock her to sleep. I moved my hands in a downward, petting motion. "There, there."

We stared at each other until Katie said, "Mama, do you know Miss Stella?"

"I did," Audrey said. "Once."

Behind the sunglasses she closed her eyes. She took a deep breath, her nostrils pinching together, and then let it out. "Jesus Christ," she said again, softly, "I can't do this right now." And she turned away.

"I'll call you," I said after her.

"Sure you will," she called back. "Come on, Katie."

"I love you," I shouted, because it seemed that was what she wanted. And because she has to answer when I call.

She shot out a hand in a short, chopping gesture, a bracelet jumping on her wrist.

Of course I'm going to call her. I want to see my grandkids grow up. I just, let's face it, don't want to be their free babysitter. Or nanny, or chauffeur, or Super Grandma with trips and planned activities and a bedroom in my house for each of them, losing my weekends and summer vacations whenever Audrey feels like she needs a break.

I raised my children. I went through that already. Now I want my own life. I didn't know how much I'd wanted that, how intensely, until thank the Lord my husband cheated and then divorced me and I had all the time in the world.

The bus is perfect. I know she's safe, I can tell you what she's wearing, I get to see her beautiful smile. Anything more than that, anything closer, and the demands would start, all the doing and the fixing and the food and the care and the worry, and my sweet, long, thoughtful days would go back to being a blur.

I watched them walk into the library, Katie holding her mother's hand. What a sweet little girl she is, so smart, so friendly. I really am proud of her. I wonder what the boy looks like, if he takes after his father or me.

I couldn't go into the library now. Audrey would just build up a head of steam, rehearsing my wrongs and short-comings, her sufferings and sacrifices, and if

I were anywhere in the vicinity, she would let loose.

I'll call. I know her number. There's a phone in the building and local calls are free. I've looked at it lots of times, thought about picking up the receiver, but then walked right past.

Because the lady was right. Sometimes you just need a little time to yourself.

A Many-Chambered Vessel

"WORST JOB YOU ever had," I say, discarding a seven.

She draws a card, places it in the holder. The table we can swing across her bed is handy; the tubes taped to her hand are not.

"Hauling irrigation pipe," she says. "They're heavy. And you have to move them every day, for potatoes."

"I hated that job too," my mom says from the couch. She's knitting a hat for the baby.

These Kellner women, hands always busy. If this were a Sunday long ago, the leftovers would be stacked in the fridge labeled with names of their owners. The dishwasher would be quietly humming, the table wiped and the floor swept, and then the cards would come out. It used to be skat but then Oma discovered Skip-Bo and Skip-Bo it's been for the last twenty years.

"Best job," I say after she's discarded a five. Her discard columns crowd the table to its rim. My field is nearly empty. I spend and she saves. She doesn't remember the Depression, but she remembers the wars. I remember the Berlin wall coming down.

When I traveled to Germany on exchange I researched our ancestry, wanting to prove to Uncle Will we didn't descend from kings. We were peasants on a medieval fief and before that we were barbarians hunting with spears. I am proud of our thick calves, our strong lungs. My mother can still carry her weight on her back. None of us broke bones, ever, until Oma fell outside the door to her apartment and lay in a pool of blood until the morning nurse found her.

"Why didn't you scream?" I demanded.

"I didn't want to bother anyone," she said.

"Best job." Her speech is slurred, but she's dressed today in one of the cotton smocks she loves to wear, the ones with the deep pockets. I've never seen her in anything else. Her hair is combed and still so much black, as black as the frame of her glasses. "The greenhouse. I used to work there in the mornings, when I was teaching, before I went to school. It was my job to water."

"What did you like about it?"

This is not the end-of-your-life talk. I hope she knows that. I'm not gathering information to tell my baby, the one sleeping under my ribs. This is the way we've always talked, over cards, washing dishes, shucking peas from her garden or cleaning blackberries from the back forty of the farm, when I was young, when I was in college and stopped by on every trip north, when I was working and stopped by less often.

Now I live too far away. We don't have Sunday dinners at my house. We need to. My daughter will need to know what Kellner women are like, how we live. She needs to learn it from the woman who taught me. Oma can't go yet.

"It was so quiet," Oma says. She frowns at a Skip-Bo like she can't remember what it means. "Everything smelled good. And when the sun came up . . ."

"I didn't know that, Mom." My mother looks up from her needles. "I thought you just waitressed." She never thought to ask any of this. There were always chores to be done.

I imagine my grandmother in the greenhouse, slender, still young despite the children, her face touched with morning glow, everything possible. She loved teaching and could grow anything; her garden was proof of that. But then Opa got injured in his janitorial job and she quit the school too in solidarity.

Just a waitress. Just a wife. Even though she worked from sunup till well past dark, running the farm, tending the animals, raising the children, and ferrying things to the man on the couch, bringing his medicines, taking away his trash. I'll never take what she did from any man, not even my husband, the father of my child. My mother never did, either. Oma did it for us so we didn't have to.

How did it not ruin her? How did it not wear her down, the relentless grind? I am ashamed of my easy life, the computer I turn off when my husband comes home, how he kisses me over dinner, brings me a book when I put my feet up and watch my ankles swell over my shoes, just as Oma's do after all those years on her feet. When she moved to the senior living complex she took up wearing slippers and she deserves that luxury, deserves much more than that, for what she has endured in her life.

"Oma. It's a Skip-Bo," I say softly as she scowls at the card. The machine beside her hisses. "Play it. You can play it anywhere."

I meet my mother's worried eyes. She won't cry, not in front of her mother, but she cried when she called me on the phone.

It wasn't a fall; it was a massive heart attack. It's the heart that takes down the Kellner women, the only thing that can. Oma's grandmother died in the fields, hoe in her hand. Her own mother's heart stopped the night before I was born, an hour before I came.

I like to think she waited to see me, waited to breathe out the wisdom I will need to survive this long life, this hardy body. Oma had cancer in the ovaries and Mom had melanoma taken off her face. I know it's waiting in me, somewhere, that tainted admixture. But we're draught horses; we work, and we endure. Oma still has her ration stamps from the war. Her house burned down as a little girl and they built it again, in brick. She buried a baby and then she buried a daughter and then she buried the husband who tried to kill her, slowly, for forty years, with his heavy hands, his sneer. Still she kept going. She won't stop until her heart does. I hope I am just like her.

She lays the Skip-Bo and then she wipes out her holder, pulling from her neat columns, tossing cards like a dealer. She lays the last and her chest sinks with a sigh. I thought her confused and she was calculating how to beat me.

"Oma, I hope my daughter is just like you."

"I'm going to take a sleep now." She pushes feebly at the table.

I clean up the game, shuffling the stacks, sliding the well-worn piles into their box. I push back the table and pull forward her water, adding ice. I look at the monitors, though my mother's been watching every pulse. What will she do without her mother? Who will she be? Why have I never asked my mother the end-of-life questions?

"I hope the baby gets your black hair, too." There's still more black in Oma's hair than white, and my mother has the same thick mane. I got my father's wispy brown hair, but you can tell I'm a Kellner. I have their shape and their steady hearts, two things I will keep to the end.

"I was so dark when I was little. Brown as a nut. They called me the Little Indian."

We've heard this before, many times. Her breathing is shallow, her eyes darting beneath the lids. She's in pain but won't tell us. She never told anyone. She knew no one could fix it. Not even when my mother called my college to say they'd finally done it, they'd taken Oma away from the farm house after they found Opa, his mind lost to dementia, threatening her with the shotgun. Not then, not in the hospital, not even when she buried him did Oma admit that man, or anything else, had hurt her.

"I always tanned so well," my mother says. "I'm glad I got your skin."

"Brown as a nut." Her fingers flutter for the blanket, as if she's weaving, and I pull up the quilt that the hospice group made her. She loves it. It's thick and heavy and patterned in black and white, just how she's lived her life.

"If you're too happy, something's missing," she told me once as we weeded her garden. "It means something doesn't matter enough."

Was she ever too happy? She's laughing in her wedding photos, the pictures of her holding her babies. I hope my daughter has her skin and that same secret smile, the curved dimple, the gleam in the eye. Maybe I shouldn't have passed down these genes, the doubled chin, the cankles. But I hope she gets that smile.

"You rest," I say, stroking the quilt over her shoulder. We're not touchers, we Kellner women, but my hands say what my words can't. "I'll run get lunch for me and Mom and your great-granddaughter. You want anything?"

"Jane was a feeder," Oma says. Her voice is raspy. She sucks at her lips. "Oh, how that child could eat."

My mother looks lost. Everything droops. A woman of a certain age. In twenty years I'll look like her, and someday I will lose her, too.

Oma's eyes open. "Connie?" she whispers, and that's when I want to cry.

It's happening. They're gathering, the ghosts. Jane was the baby she buried too young, then my aunt Connie's heart gave out on the warehouse floor. I missed her funeral; I was in Germany at the time, walking the paths of our ancestors. Opa's death didn't feel like a loss, the removal of that strange cursing man on the couch, satisfied by nothing. Oma is my pillar, the ruler by which I measure everything. She taught me how to mop a floor, make a pie crust, remove a splinter without breaking the tip.

I hold the hand that is free of tubes and put my other hand on my belly. "I'm going to name her Ida, after you," I whisper. "Ida, baby, this is your Oma. Say hi."

I can't say goodbye. I want the dignity of a formal parting, confession, absolution, all of it. But my heart is bursting in my mouth. I press my hand to her shoulder, that valiant rise and fall, and we breathe those last few breaths together.

"We'll see you soon," I say.

My mother tells me to stop by Oma's and bring back another pair of slippers. She wants an Arby's sandwich, roast beef. I nod as though this is just our afternoon. She hugs me carefully around my belly, eager for what's inside. I love to think what she will mean to my own daughter, me the sturdy link between them, passing down the strength and the secret.

I'm in the parking lot when my mother calls. Oma is gone. She slipped out the window while I walked down the stairs, gifting me with her last breath, making space in the world for my child to be born.

I sit in the garage and cry till I'm empty. And then I put the car in gear. I have to eat, and so does my mother, the one who will bear everything that comes next. Kellner women keep moving even when the blow goes deep. My daughter will learn this.

I used to think it was plodding animal ignorance, the inheritance of our German peasantry, brute strength, spoiled blood. Now I realize it was rage. Rage kept her heart beating, made her sharp at cards and everything else. When the rage faltered she began to shrink, not knowing who she was anymore.

I will see her again. In the days to come I will see her everywhere, and even years later I will catch her when I sink my hands in a pie crust, when I smell blackberries, when my daughter flashes that smile. I will teach my daughter how to mop floors, remove splinters, shuck peas. I will want her to be happy and watch to see if it's too much, if something's missing. I will tell her that what we make and what we pass on last long after we do. And that the scars from her many-times broken heart are the signs that she has lived.

Married, Living in Italy

You'd adore Carlito, the fruit vendor down the street. He calls all the women bella *and makes wine from his very own vineyard. Plus he sells this prosciutto and mozzarella sandwich that I could eat every day. I'm thinking of getting a motorbike—everyone here has one—though Ma would have a seizure, I know. Tuscany is so beautiful it's a cliché. No wonder all the rich Americans are lining up to buy a villa and live* la dolce vita. *I'll call soon.* Te amo. *Lonnie.*

I can't send this postcard because I haven't figured out how to fake an international postmark without getting into trouble with the U.S. Postal Service. Nana has a stack of mail waiting for her, thick as my hand is wide, dating back to my last birthday. On the phone my mother wants to know, "Why don't you write your grandmother? You know she never checks that e-mail account you set up for her. A poor, lonely old woman."

Nana volunteers at the library, cooks for Meals on Wheels, and babysits her friends' great-grandchildren. She runs the card games, the secret Santa drawings, and the weekly Bible study at Shady Acres. I don't think she has time to read mail. My aunt teases her that if she ever sat for more than five minutes without knitting as she did the crossword, her head would explode.

"Let me talk to Fernando," my mother says. A car drives by blasting Katy Perry, and I try to shield the cell phone so my mother won't hear. What I should do is stream an Italian talk show on my laptop and call her from my apartment. But I like to leave my apartment as often as possible.

"Fernando's not here. He's talking to a realtor about the house we want to buy."

"Ooh," my mother says. "One of those palaces you see in the movies? With all the windows, and the statues out front?"

"Sure, we can afford a palazzo on my salary."

"Aren't you scared the whole thing's going to sink right into the water?"

"I live in Florence, Ma. Florence. Not Venice."

"Hmm." The food processor spurts, and then she says, "So I've been looking at plane tickets home and March seems a good time . . ."

"I'll check, but I don't know if I'll have any time off in March."

"Oh. Okay." The food processor whines again, and then she says, brightly, "We could come visit you in Italy? For your birthday?" I know she gets a weekly e-mail on discount fares, because she passes those e-mails on to me.

"Ah. That's a great idea. But don't book anything just yet. Maybe wait till the house thing goes through?" I sound just like Nana. Oh, I wouldn't want to put anybody out . . .

"Tell Fernando to talk to your father. Your father knows plenty about real estate."

My father works at the First National Bank of Omaha selling mortgages to first-time home buyers. He has been employed by this bank for thirty-five years and has, every day of his working life, begun the morning by getting coffee from the vending machine and sharpening his pencils, one by one.

I hear a recorded voice informing me that I have ten seconds left on my card. "I have to go, Ma. My phone's going to cut out in a second."

"Call me tomorrow, before my soaps start," she shouts over the sound of the food processor. "Eleven."

"I will." My good-bye is drowned out by a metallic click.

Carlito watches me as I walk into his store, this indispensable little deli that sells day-old fruit and sandwiches, four kinds of soup, and various dry and perishable goods. I like finding cheese and bread stacked next to lighter fluid and a tiny package of sandpaper. Carlito brings order to an otherwise formless universe.

"*Ciao, bella,*" he says when I come in. He takes a long puff on his pipe, blowing a ring of smoke across the No Smoking sign above the counter which is required, by city ordinance and New York state law, to be there. The whole store smells of aged tobacco, like grandfathers and used bookstores.

"*Como sta?* Looking for another phone card? A sandwich? *Vino rosso?*" He nods toward the vending machine in one corner, crammed between the ATM and a freezer full of beer and wine. It would cost me 49 cents a minute to call to Mexico, $1.49 to France, and $1.57 a minute to Italy. Or from Italy.

"I'm looking for dinner," I tell him, prowling down the aisle with the boxed foods. I try not to look at the macaroni and cheese. Thinking about mac and cheese makes me think about Adam, and thinking about Adam makes my stomach hurt.

"Call a boyfriend," Carlito says. "Have him take you out to dinner."

"There is no boyfriend, Carlito, I'm sorry to say."

He shakes his head, reaches up to stroke the glossy line of his salt-and-pepper hair. Carlito is of that cast of thinking—and he is not alone—that a woman is not a fully realized being until she has acquired a mate.

"I saw someone going into your apartment just yesterday, *si?*"

"That was maintenance. My toilet backed up

again." I'll have to put that in the next postcard to Nana. *Problems with the plumbing, but you know these centuries-old palazzos!*

The overhead lights buzz and the flickering hurts my eyes. Outside the trees are entering the sharp and naked phase of fall, and night comes early in these northern lands. All that awaits me at home, in my apartment down the street, are piles of museum journals, cockroaches, some wilting ivy, and an indifferent cat.

The view out my bedroom window is of the fourth-floor landing of the building next to mine. In the months since I moved to Albany, I've never seen anyone pass back or forth in that stairwell. Yet all over the world, people come home to families, homes, lives. Not in an alternate universe, but in this one.

"Tell me something, Carlito. What does Fernando mean in Italian?"

"Is a Spanish name," he grunts, flipping through his copy of *La Repubblica.*

"But of Latin derivation, right?"

"Wrong peninsula. You are thinking of Fernando the bull, *si?*"

"Ferdinand," I correct him, but he's chuckling to himself. This is a new low, even for me: I've invented my lover from a Walt Disney cartoon.

AFTER CARLITO and my boss, the only other person in Albany with whom I have regular conversations is the guy at the post office who helped me set up my PO box. Now he watches me every time I come in, as if suspicious that I'll be careless with USPS property. I'll never tell him getting mail is the highlight of my day. Some things only work in conversation when they're not true.

"What is it today?" he says as I plop another

overstuffed enveloped onto his scale. I've reinforced the corners with duct tape, our running joke. "Pulitzer prize winner? Steamy historical romance?"

"Corrected proofs for the State Historical Society's annual magazine. Only slightly less titillating."

"Do I get a copy? Lonnie." He tacks on the last after taking a prolonged look at the return address. If he looks too hard at the To address of the other envelope he might get the idea that I really am interested in the fishing history of the Hudson River, and that would be unfortunate.

I give his name tag a hard stare. "Maybe. Lloyd."

He's got a funny smile, one that looks like he's tucking his lips in. "The nametag isn't mine. I lost mine. We keep extras sitting around in case Quality Control comes in."

I look again: wiry guy, tall and lean as a whip, wispy brown hair and a lazy left eye behind rimless glasses. The superheroes always hide behind glasses. "Listen, can I ask a question?"

"Sure, if I can ask you mine first. Insurance or tracking?" Behind the funny smile is a great set of teeth.

"Tracking, please." I beam at him, feeling prosperous. The museum will reimburse me for postage. "Can you make it look like I'm sending a letter from Italy?"

"What?" His fingers flex in the air before his touch screen. "Why?"

Why? I was traveling in Italy, I could say. I told friends and loved ones I'd send postcards and couldn't find a drop box, and now I want to make it look like they came from Europe. I'd hate to disappoint the family.

"What?" Lloyd says again.

"Okay, I have to send some mail—actually a lot of

mail—to my grandma, and she thinks I'm living in Florence. Italy."

His eyes read my face like a antique typewriter cartridge, scanning back and forth. "Let me think about that," he says, slaps the postage sticker on my envelope, and slides it into the bin. "Debit or credit?"

I can feel the shorter hairs around my face sticking straight up. I can feel my pores.

While Lloyd thinks, I check my post office box. The mail is all the same. Catalog for clothing I can't afford. Rejection letter from Smithsonian about internship. Application for credit card encouraging me to spend money I don't have. Letter from the Met saying they don't have open positions at this time.

The last envelope is of that thick creamy paper used for résumés, the kind I buy when I'm trying to sell an article to a history journal. It's addressed to Miss Lenore Whitterling and the return address is Mrs. Kenneth Larch.

I know that name. The buzzing from the fluorescent lights sounds like a swarm of deranged locusts.

Mrs. Kenneth Larch—Miss Amanda Keyes, when I knew her—was president of my Westside High School class, though she belonged at the prep school and never let us middle-class scrubs forget it. Good grades, community service at the nursing home, star of the girls tennis team, and Miss Council Bluffs for three years running though she didn't actually live there.

The enclosed letter is a colorful but grammatically flawed invitation to our ten-year class reunion, coaxing me to pull out those stone-washed jeans and leg warmers for a great bash at the country club where her father, it so happens, is a long-standing member. Maybe Miss Amanda Prom Queen Keyes can still fit into her little size four miniskirts, but some of us haven't been size four since we were twelve.

The RSVP card has happy faces and sad faces next to the options and inquires, "What have you been up to? Tell us where you are now!"

I send a quick glance around the room. Lloyd stamps a box brought in by an older man. A shabby teenager tries to get stamps out of the vending machine without putting in the proper change. A woman I've seen in my building browses the wall of commemorative stamps, stroking the ones with kittens and puppies. Wouldn't Mrs. Kenneth Larch love this.

The reply postcard is carnation pink. No doubt these little rectangles will be tacked up on some huge equally pink poster at the reunion, like sprinkles on a cake. I can just imagine what Amanda's will say:

"After I got my degree in social work at the Very Elite Private Woman's College, I took a job at the State Welfare Agency and founded a program to place orphans in foster homes. Five years ago I married Ken, whom you all remember as second-string quarterback for the Huskers, and our son Cody will be two in November. Ken is an associate partner in the law firm Smugly & Snoot, and on the weekends we like to go waterskiing at our little cabin on the lake." Happy face, happy face, hearts.

I would like to see Amanda's reaction to my scrawl. "M.A. in communication theory and M.S. in urban studies from University of Omaha." I sound like a nerd. "M.S. in museum studies at Lincoln. Working on certificate in public history from University of Albany." I *am* a nerd. "Underemployed." Too acidic. "Giving tours of the Albany Institute to bored retirees and obnoxious middle school students, living with cockroaches, rejection letters, and failed ambitions." Too long. I could try being direct, for once: "Broke and broken-hearted in New York."

I can already hear the exclamations from the planning committee: "Lonnie Whitterling! Didn't you just know she'd move to New York?"

"I don't think I remember her," one will say.

"You don't? How could you forget her? She was class valedictorian."

"Oh?" another will say. "Who did she go out with?"

"Hmm," Mrs. Larch will say, tapping her little chin. "You know, I don't think she went out with anybody."

I grab my marker and put a big black X next to the regrets box. In the lines provided I write in bold capitals: MARRIED. LIVING IN ITALY.

I march to the counter and hand Lloyd the card. He reads it and stares at me, at least with one eye; the left one looks over my shoulder. He's in two places at once, here and elsewhere. I know how I look to him: short girl, dumpy figure, neglected haircut, freckled nose. Great sense of humor, though. This is the part where he goes and talks to his supervisor and I hear about how tampering with U.S. mail is a federal offense.

"Can I ask you something?" Lloyd says.

"What now?" I say, readying myself for the speech.

"Would you like to go to dinner sometime?"

MOVING TO ITALY is the most creative thing I've ever done. It's too expensive for my mother to call. Florence was apt if unimaginative, the first thing that came into my head. My mother figures I'm every bit as safe in Italy as I was giving tours of the Historic Mile in Florence, Nebraska.

I started out living with some friends from graduate school but then along came Fernando, who is a sensitive, dark-haired architect. I did see him originally as a fashion designer, but my mother would have found that inexplicable since I never showed the slightest interest in fashion while I was growing up.

Dear Nana:
You'd love my neighbor, Senora Lorenzo, who lives downstairs. She used to be an opera singer. She wakes me up every morning singing – she goes through about an opera a week. This week we're on Carmen. She has the most jewelry of anyone I know, including Aunt Joan. I wish you could meet her.

Now, that raises all sorts of interesting possibilities. Nana getting this postcard, me getting Nana out of Nebraska, getting any or all of us to Italy.

Mrs. Larsen catches me on the stairs as I leave that morning. She flings open the door of her ground-floor apartment and comes out to meet me wearing her dressing gown, a plastic pink shower cap, and sparkly black slippers with heels.

"Don't look at my hair, it's a mess," she says, patting the curlers under her cap. "Do you want to come in? I'm baking cookies."

I point at the toilet brush in her hand. "That doesn't say 'baking' to me."

She laughs. Music—possibly from Carmen, I wouldn't know—pours out of the kitchen, and I smell cinnamon and cooking spray. "Oh, you know Mary comes to clean."

Mary, as far as I can tell, is her daughter. Mrs. Larsen is always talking about Mary this, Mary that, when Mary was here, though I've never seen the woman. Curled hair and fresh makeup every morning, a brooch pinned at her throat, Mrs. Larsen makes more of an effort for a day spent in her apartment than I do for work.

"I'm on my way out the door," I say. "Shall I stop by later?"

"Oh, are you going to work? I suppose most girls do these days. Mary works in a law office, you know. But you're not wearing that, are you? Do you want to borrow a scarf?" She surveys me from my scruffy toes to the top of my hair which, I'm afraid, is frizzing in the dry air. "A choker? A bracelet? You're not even wearing a skirt."

"I move around a lot at work." This is my fate: I will always be scrutinized by the Amanda Larches of the world and found lacking.

"Hmm." She touches my face for a moment and then, to my surprise, leans forward and gives me a motherly kiss. "Have a good day, dear," she says, and shoos me out the door with a half moon of pink lipstick printed on my cheek.

Dear Nana,
I haven't told you yet about my job: I give tours of old houses.

Nana never understood what I do even when I was doing it back in Nebraska. Museum studies seemed to her something people do when they're retired and their real work in the world is done. She would laugh to see me here, sitting behind a desk in what used to be somebody's home, giving morning tours to attention-deficit or special-needs grade school classes and giving the afternoon eyeball to young kids cutting class and trying to sneak into the greenhouse to make out. Nana could never sit still for that long.

But Omaha kicked me out. First with the city budget crunch they scaled back tours everywhere, Joslyn Castle, Freedom Park, and I lost my cushy by-appointment-only job giving tours at the Gottlieb mansion. Then I started losing crucial motor skills. I pulled out in front of other drivers in traffic without seeing the car. The wrong people picked up when I made phone calls. I developed a habit of counting things, windows on buildings, the lines on my knuckles. One night alone in my apartment, when the lid wouldn't twist off, I opened a jar of olives by dropping it on the floor. Shattering glass makes a very satisfying sound, despite the clean-up that follows. I realized Omaha was going to close in on me and shut out the simplest things, like my sanity, or having somebody to talk to during commercial breaks.

The goodbyes were neither drawn-out nor painful. My mother came around quickly, more interested than anxious. My best friend hugged me and said "I'll miss you" and Adam sent a heartless e-mail: "Heard your moving, sounds great, hope all goes well. Take care adam." I couldn't believe I was still pining for a man who couldn't spell. Finished, I said to myself as I drove away with the rented van that wheezed up every hill in western Pennsylvania. Over. Done. *Finito.*

And all tied up neatly, except I had told everyone I was going to Albany for a few weeks to stay with friends, and then moving to Italy.

It's true what they say, that Italian men are unbelievably good-looking. I get proposed to on the street just like Mom did years ago. Remember that story?

My mom went to Italy once, in college. An Italian guy asked her to marry him while she was taking a photo of the Arch of Constantine. He pulled the car over to the sidewalk where she stood with her friends and told her she was the most beautiful woman he'd ever seen.

"I could have accepted that proposal I got in

Rome," she tells my father sometimes while she stands at the kitchen counter chopping carrots. "I could be married and living in Italy."

And my dad, comfortable in his armchair in the living room, always answers, "Marcia, you don't speak Italian."

It's two o'clock, and right on schedule, Romeo and Juliet wander in the door. They've been kicked out before, so now they're doing recon to see who's at the desk. I've not misnamed them; she looks to be about fourteen. I should threaten to call their parents. But something about their clasped hands makes me look away; that glimmer of new-found love shows on their faces, that discovery of something no one else has so deeply experienced in the entire history of the human race.

It makes my stomach curl, much like standing on the edge of a cliff. I remember the first night Adam and I drove home together after a late movie. He'd smuggled in a flask of rum and Coke and I had to drive his car, a Honda Civic and a stick shift. In front of my door he put his cold hands on my ears and, very seriously, kissed me. He smelled like evening dew on fresh-cut grass. I didn't know you could crave a smell like that, or starve from the lack of it.

The lie grew out of embarrassment, when my mother sounded so excited and hopeful when I called her. She imagined a fresh new start, me casting off the shackles of ennui, or disillusionment, or whatever it was that had kept her straight-A daughter indoors eating Klondike bars and watching Netflix originals. She imagined I was finding myself, finding the life she had always dreamed of, the life she might have had if she'd taken that Italian man up on his offer.

Then I incorporated Fernando into the mix, when I got tired of the hints about whether I was meeting any of those handsome Florentine men. After that she was so happy I could see her glow of approval all the way from New York. It lit up the whole western sky.

My dad, I'm sure, would be fine with whatever I chose to do. He says, "Don't worry about her, Marcia; she'll find her feet." He's got an original Bank of Florence $1 bill framed on his wall because he says the girl in the picture looks like me, the same black hair, round chin, pointy nose. But I knew that every time I got turned down for a job, or stopped dating a boy she'd liked, my mother laid awake at night reviewing each moment in her history of raising me, trying to figure out where she went wrong.

Still waiting to get an interview at the Uffizi. How I'd love to be able to wander at twilight through all those wide, soaring rooms.

Will call soon. Miss you. Love, Lonnie.

I add a few X's and O's at the bottom. One of the older volunteers wanders out of the sitting room where he was guarding the candlesticks, looks at me writing, sniffs to himself, and then heads for the greenhouse. Romeo and Juliet have had it for the day. And so have I; I have to get to the post office before it closes. I tuck the postcard into my bag as though I have every intention of mailing it.

I invented Italy so my mother wouldn't worry. I invented Fernando so she could sleep at night. But sometimes, when I'm in bed and the clock says 3:00 am for the fourteenth night in a row, I imagine that sound in the hall is Adam coming up the stairs to tell me he's finally figured things out, that I'm the woman he wants to be with. And even now, with all this distance, I'm still not sure I wouldn't do anything he wanted. Lie down, roll over. Play dead.

"I CAN'T PUT a fake postmark on your letters," Dave—not Lloyd—says when I come in. Apparently he found his real nametag. "Tampering with U.S. mail is a federal offense."

"Oh, come on." I drop another envelope on his scale and try to smile winningly. "I'll pay for the real postage. I'll even pay extra for the fake stamps. Just postmark it Firenze.""

"I can't. And even if I could, I still don't get why your grandma thinks you live in Florence," Lloyd—I mean Dave—says. "How did she get that idea?"

"Can you just show me what the stamp looks like? Maybe I could draw it on the postcards. That would be enough to satisfy my mother."

"And get you thrown in jail." He puts his elbows on the counter, props his chin, and stares at me with his good eye. "So your mother thinks you live in Italy, too?"

"Who's to say I didn't just get back from Italy?" None of this is his business.

"Is Lonnie even your real name?"

"My mother named me Lenore. Don't ask."

I realize that in our conversation I have been touching my chin and throat. In the communications textbooks that indicates you are insecure or feeling vulnerable. In the women's magazines it means you are trying to attract a mate. I lower my hand in case he's read either of these manuals and thinks I am doing this on purpose. I hear a clatter that says I just knocked over the display about the U.S. government savings bonds.

Dave grins as I bend down, flustered. I'm beginning to like that crooked smile, higher on one side, and the way his short brown hair sticks up in the back. The nerve signals in my fingers aren't reaching my brain. Is he going to try to kiss me? We're alone in the post office, which somehow feels sexier than being alone anywhere else. We could sneak into the back room and make out on the sorting table.

I may be rushing things, since he hasn't followed up on that dinner invitation yet.

"Why'd you leave Omaha?" he wants to know.

I'm not going to tell him that I had become afraid of myself. If it suddenly seemed rational to open a jar of olives by dropping it on the floor, what was to keep me from tracking down Adam and his new girlfriend at the Antiquarian Bookstore and making a scene?

"Who wouldn't want to move to this fair city? Albany, the promised land?"

He crooks one eyebrow.

"There's a public history program at the university that offers an advanced certificate." So much for preserving my mystery. "And, well, I might have needed some distance from an ex."

I want to ask him about his exes, the women he's loved, what it takes to become one of them. Without instigation a silent movie plays in my head, grainy photos, characters moving jerkily like puppets on a string. Adam somewhere, lounging against a door, cool and inaccessible, holding a cigarette; me circling around, aching, asking for a light.

What I would have said to the girlfriend is, have you figured out yet he's a block of ice? That things come in, but they don't actually touch him? You think he's looking at you, but he's looking far past you, thinking about something else.

Dave looks like he could never be cool about anything. He has warm-looking skin.

"I'm not taking you to dinner in that shirt," Dave says, indicating my Scott Residence Hall T-shirt with its slogan. Omaha, Go Against the Flow.

"I have eight of these, in different colors. And

nothing else." I can hear my mother groaning all the way from Nebraska.

"Fine. I'll take you to the Dinosaur BBQ up in Troy. You'll fit right in. Where should I pick you up? Your place?"

"Ah, no." My mother would screech, but my mother comes from the days when being careful meant making the required number of trips to the powder room to ensure you didn't have a shiny nose. I don't think my mother dated anyone but my father, and Nana didn't date at all. My grandpa saw her in church at a funeral and fell in love with her on the spot. He approached her father after the service and came over that night for dinner. Three months later, after a proper mourning period was observed, they married and out of convenience, or passion, or sheer habit, neither of them ever looked at anyone else.

"I'll meet you here," I say.

"At eight," he says. "Practice your Italian."

As I wait for the bus I realize I am standing in the center of a concrete square as though floating on an island, alone and untouched. I want to tell my mother about Dave, about the way he talks with his hands, about that foolish moment when we both just stared at each other. How I wish I could come to him with an uncluttered past. I wonder if all women feel this, that their old lovers follow them even into new places, their faces like the smile of the Cheshire cat grinning obscenely from the branches of winter-bare trees, watching from brick windowsills like a lingering conscience. My square of sidewalk is surrounded by many other concrete squares of sidewalk and I don't know what would bridge that space.

MRS. LARSEN, I learn, was a knockout when she was younger. A bona fide bombshell. She worked as a showgirl in a high-class casino in Atlantic City. She shows me a picture of her in costume, a few square inches of beads and yellow feathers, most of them piled in a foot-and-a-half-high headdress sprouting plastic rubies and ostrich plumes. She had Audrey Hepburn's cheekbones and Marlene Dietrich's lips. She must have made poor old Mr. Larsen's eyes goggle right out of his head.

Then she shows me pictures of Mary. Mary didn't inherit any of her mother's knockoutedness. She looks like she resented that fact, too, always scowling in the photos, low-browed, bearing an unfortunately prominent replica of Mr. Larsen's nose.

"She looks very self-possessed," I say politely. "She takes after Mr. Larsen, I bet."

Mrs. Larsen giggles, tugs at her pink shower cap, pulls another framed photograph off the mantel from behind a crowd of coupon flyers, old phone bills, and variously colored wads of Kleenex which appear to be handled but not used. Mr. Larsen is younger in this one, his straight dark eyebrows and heavy nose suggesting strength of character rather than ill humor.

"Handsome devil," I reply, not entirely lying.

"The fights we used to have!" Mrs. Larsen dusts the glass with a handy Kleenex. "He tried to break up with me once at a restaurant in Jersey City. He was walking out the door. I picked up my sandwich and I threw it at him, from three tables away. And it hit him, did it ever! Right on the back of the neck."

"What did he do?" I try to imagine being in this restaurant, eating my lunch, watching this happen. I try to imagine being the kind of woman who could launch a sandwich across a room at a departing lover, and with accuracy, no less.

"What did he do?" She laughs. "He wiped the sauce off his neck and licked his fingers. And then he started laughing! You could hear the whole restaurant breathe a sigh of relief. And then he ran to me and swooped me up and twirled me around, and we went home, and—well." She whirls around, picture in hand, as if to demonstrate. "And then he asked me to marry him."

I put out a hand, fearing the spins will become dangerous, but she keeps her feet. "A brute of a man," she says. "But he had his moments." She puts the portrait back on the shelf.

"What kind of sandwich was it?"

"Roast beef." She giggles.

I clear my throat of its lump of dust. I'll never have that bio, but it's hardly something you can feel sorry about. "Well, since you cooked, it's my job to clean up, right?"

"Oh, Mary will do it when she comes, never you fear." Mrs. Larsen wraps a clutch of cookies, sending pink sprinkles sailing in every direction. "Such a good girl," she says, picking up a platter, which I don't think I've washed yet, and nestling it in the china cabinet. "She tells me everything."

Watching Mrs. Larsen buzz around the kitchen makes me ache for my own Nana, the Bingo Queen of Shady Acres. I wish she could be here with me, one live thing in my apartment besides an inert cat and the wilting plants. I wish my mother could visit. I wish all three of us could be in Italy, sipping a cappuccino under an awning in the Piazza della Signoria, flipping coins into the Neptune Fountain and admiring David's enormous stone hands. Mrs. Larsen could come too. What a tableau we would make: the mother, the wise women, and the battle maiden who fights in armor, the huntress Diana who flees from the touch of a man.

When the kitchen is sparkling, Mrs. Larsen presses

the packet of cookies into my hand. She's used freezer paper and masking tape. I hear sprinkles skidding around inside. "For your postman," she says. "It never hurts to woo a man with sweets."

I accept the cookies and start on my way up the stairs. It never hurts to take advice from a woman who, in her prime, was Scarlett O'Hara armed with red lipstick and birth control.

"Lenore! Lenore! Lenore!" Mrs. Larsen sticks her head out of her doorway and chimes my name like an invocation. When I look back at her, she gives me a wave, the bracelets on her wrist jangling. "Your mama raised you right!"

I want to hold her elbows gently, like pockets. I want to be somebody's Mary. I want for once to see the inside of somebody's life besides my own.

All I can do is smile down the banister at her. "If there's one thing we Midwestern girls know how to do, it's clean."

ON THE FOURTH floor, I open my door to the waiting vacancy. I don't have the energy to be disgusted by the roach scuttling away. I wonder if this is how my grandmother feels when she comes back from evening cards or a trip to the grocery store. But Nana's always giving lifts or running errands for the "older folks" in her senior living complex. She's the social hub of her building, the telegraph office for all messages and news; she rules the card table the way Carlito rules his corner store. And what do I have? Fake postcards to her. I tell the lies the ways I've crowded the furniture into my apartment, trying to simulate fullness, while underneath, the walls are still white and bare.

I pour myself a glass of wine. I pull out my stash of postcards.

I have nothing to say.

I look at the clock again. The ticks clang in the incredible silence. From the bedroom comes a faint high whine, the cat snoring. I can hear the hum of refrigerators from every apartment on this floor, smell the lemony odor of the latest visit from the exterminator. In Omaha it's five in the afternoon and my mother is turning off the daytime drama and glancing at the clock, trying to decide whether she should mash the potatoes or bake them. Adam is calling his latest girlfriend from work and planning to meet his friends at one of the bars in Old Market and under the table she'll hook her foot around his ankle like I used to do. My mother thinks it's midnight in Florence and I'm strolling across the Ponte Vecchio, moonlight on the Arno, Fernando's fingers curled into mine as we talk about our new home and the Accademia, our heads filled with Donatello and ancient Italic romance.

I change my shirt after all, to a nice blouse I owned before Adam. I'm trying to resurrect something, my own innocence maybe, before my life came to this, narrowed down to this single point, one static color, a temperature at which life can survive, but barely.

I pet the cat and pull on a jacket and lock my door, hoping that when I come back, something would have changed. Anything.

DAVE SAYS there's a two hour wait for a table at the Dinosaur BBQ, and maybe we should just stay in town. Already the mark of a great personality divide: Dave thinks to call ahead. We get pizza at I Love New York and then take a walk through a sleepy downtown that has buttoned itself up for the evening, braced against the cold. We wander through the historic district so I can show him where I work. "Too bad you can't write about this to your grandmother," he says.

I trip, but he makes no move to grab my hand, or my arm. Thinking of Nana makes me think of Nana's old house, back when Pap was alive, the red blanket she draped over the living room couch, the color of sun-dried tomatoes. It was ancient and soft and worn through in spots, with tassels all around the edges. I would steal it and go build a fort in her bedroom, sit in there drawing pictures and pretending I was anything, a Cro-Magnon in my cave, an Egyptian slave painting murals in the pharaoh's tomb. Nana would find me and peer inside with gentle wonder: what are you doing in there?

"Say something to me in Italian," Dave says.

"Lei è uno scaricatore di porto," I say, which is all I remember from the wicked Italian phrasebook my college roommate bought me as a joke.

"I'm so sexy you can't stand it?"

"I told you you're a dockworker. But I used the polite form of address."

Dave stops halfway across the bridge and puts his elbows on the brickwork. He lines up a little piece of stone atop the concrete and then flicks it into the Hudson. It lands with a soft blip.

"Why fake a life?" he says. "Why not just have a real one?"

He's not looking at me. He flicks his finger and another stone cartwheels into the water.

"What's the difference? It's just a story. A little joke with my family. It's not hurting anyone."

You expect too much, my mother always said to me, after every break-up, every failed romantic hope. Too much, Lonnie. No one can live up to you.

But she's wrong. I never expect anything. Except to end up here eventually, standing in the beginnings of a cold fog, the chill wind grasping my ankles. Only this time, I don't think I can bear it.

"Now where are you going?" he says. "Running away again?"

"I'm going to stand here and fight with you? I'm not five."

"We're having a conversation," he says, his long legs keeping pace with me. "I'm asking you questions."

I turn to look at him. His glasses hold the gleam of reflected light, like Saturn through a low-grade telescope. It occurs to me that fighting can mean fixing something, a sandwich thrown across a restaurant like a bridge, two people setting up their blanket fort against the world.

"Why Italy?" He says. "Why not Turkey? Or China? Or Peru?" The wind does a mad dance through his hair. One eye looks, as usual, over my left shoulder. The other, trained on my face, doesn't look contrite in the least. He crosses his arms over his chest, a hostile gesture, self-protecting, indicating retreat. Then I realize that my arms are clasped over my chest and he's mirroring me, picking up on my body language without even realizing it. The tips of my ears tingle with cold.

"I'm freezing. I'm going home."

"I'll walk you," he says casually, as if that's something guys still do these days.

The sharp air is making my nose run. "Fine," I tell him, though at the moment I have no intention of letting him up the stairs. "But don't ask to use the toilet. And I hope you're allergic to cats."

THERE IS A strange silence in the foyer when we enter, Dave one step behind me. It's silent at any other time, but something doesn't feel right. I draw my foot back to give the double doors another kick and Dave stops me, head cocked.

"Shush," he says. "Don't you feel it? Something isn't right."

I stare at him. I've found the one man in the world who says "shush."

There's a dull thump from inside the nearest apartment, and he's at the door before I take a breath. "Hello?" He pounds on it. "Hello? Is everything all right in there?"

"That's Mrs. Larsen's," I say. "Don't bang like that. You'll scare her."

We stare at each other in the ominous silence. I swear I can see the hair rising on the back of his neck.

He turns to the door and bangs again. "Mrs. Larsen! Lonnie's here. Can you come to the door?"

The sounds we hear next I've only ever heard on TV: breaking dishes, shattering glass, and something solid hitting the floor. There is no human sound to accompany it. Dave twists the doorknob, but of course it's locked.

"I'm counting to three, and then I'm coming in," Dave shouts. I clap a hand over my mouth so I don't laugh out loud. It's not funny; I don't know why I'm laughing.

"She'll have the deadbolt on," I say, but when he reaches the count of three he heaves his shoulder against the door, and the hollow wood flings open. Dave lurches inward, almost sprawling on his face.

I swim in behind him, already in shock. There are newspapers everywhere, tissue paper, toilet paper, streamers trailing on the floor. Cups and saucers and glassware line the table, some of them broken, like a Mad Hatter tea party. I expect Mrs. Larsen to turn around, her head lifted as in her old dancing days, her expression surprised and sternly dignified. But one of the kitchen chairs has tipped over, and lying next to it, with the end of her feather boa dripping over a chair leg, is Mrs. Larsen, her face as purple as grape Kool-Aid.

"I just cleaned this kitchen," I whisper.

"Call an ambulance," Dave says from the floor.

"She's not—? She's all right. Tell me she's all right. Right?" I am not hysterical. I can babble but I will not be hysterical.

"I think it's a heart attack," he says. "Or a stroke."

"Okay. I'll call her daughter too. Mary, her number's around here somewhere—Oh, God—"

He's got a finger in her mouth. Checking the airway. I remember this from seventh grade health class. We only watched the tape on how to revive people; we never actually had to practice. "Wouldn't you think the number would be right here on the fridge?"

"The ambulance, sweetheart. Call the ambulance first," Dave says evenly, and bends his head. "And then tell me what time it is."

I'm ashamed to say that as I stand there watching with the ambulance on its way that I'm thinking of nothing noble or profound: not of the passionate, desperate beauty we find in life when it comes down to one final moment; not of the lyricism of this movement, the slow, waltzing bend of Dave's light brown head as he breathes into Mrs. Larsen's mouth.

I'm thinking of the picture of Mrs. Larsen in her chorus girl outfit, that smile, that confidence in her perfect body. I'm thinking of the way my mother must have laughed when the stranger under the Arch of Constantine proposed to her. How Nana must have felt all those afternoons in warm light, standing at the stove in her apron, knowing her children and husband were on their way home to her. How these must be the moments our mind clings to right before the end, before the silence, before the terrible, graceful light.

I shudder when I hear a rib crack. My knees dissolve.

"Count for me, Lonnie," Dave says, watching Mrs. Larsen's face. So I kneel on the floor and count seconds, and he alternates breathing and compressions just the way we were taught in health class, and even though I'm counting it feels like no time is passing, that we are suspended here, frozen, on a cold terrazzo floor.

When the screech of the ambulance cuts off and the paramedics rush in, I come partway out of the trance. I feel the jolt of the defibrillator in my own chest. Every nerve in my body is bent on this one desire. I've never wanted anything so much in my life—not even Adam—as much as I want Mrs. Larsen to breathe.

Then the lines on the monitor give a great leap and Mrs. Larsen's heart takes off like a Husker going for the goal line. Somebody cheers; it's probably me. The blue-uniformed paramedics bustle over her, wrapping her in blankets, getting her on a stretcher, getting the stretcher on the cart. Dave speaks their language, some abbreviated, code-like words. "Contact family?" the older one questions as they exit, and Dave nods.

He picks up broken glass while I make the call. Mary is as querulous over the phone as I imagined she would be from her picture. She acts like I'm a robber who broke into the apartment. I know she's going to drive all the way over here trying to decide who to sue. If she snipes at Dave I'm going to punch her right in the middle of Mr. Larsen's nose.

I walk into Mrs. Larsen's room to pack her an overnight bag. She'll need underwear, toothbrush, magazines. I'm intruding into the most intimate part of her life. She has a decorating style I don't agree with, involving lots of knickknacks and lace, but there's a charm to it, a blooming pink warmth. It's a home someone would come home to.

I hear Dave dealing with voices in the hall, curious neighbors, ambulance chasers, Carlito asking the name of the hospital they've taken her to. Mrs. Larsen's bedroom also looks into the stairwell of the next building, but on this floor someone has put a potted plant in the window, a sign of habitation. A fat purple blossom balances on its stem.

Somewhere between collecting crumpled newspaper and winding up rolls of streamers, the shock hits me. If Mrs. Larsen makes it to the hospital, if she needs this overnight bag, there will be things I can't imagine happening to her, surgeries, medications, complications. It's possible that what comes out from under that blue sheet will be unrecognizable. Who would have found her if the night had been warmer, if Dave and I had still been walking on the other side of the river, trading insults? Who might or might not walk by my Nana's apartment at just the right time?

I sink to the floor and lean against the refrigerator. I like that it feels warm despite being an appliance made to cool things. I like that my shoulder blades feel the hum.

Dave stands at the sink drinking red fruit punch out of a plastic pitcher. It stains his mouth to the color of a fresh bruise. I watch his throat moving as the liquid volume of the juice pitcher shrinks. I want to kiss him as soon as possible, but I'm afraid I will feel Mrs. Larsen's purple lips on his red ones.

"I need to make a call," I hear myself saying. I think that if I went upstairs right now the pile of postcards to Nana would fall on me with a hundred tiny mouths and tear me to pieces.

Dave wipes his mouth on his sleeve, leaving a long smear, then hands me the cordless phone.

His fingers brushing mine startle me with their reminder of material substance. One minute he was a man walking down a cobbled street and in the next he was doing CPR. He's like a miracle, only real, a saint with pizza sauce on his knee.

I let the phone dangle for a moment from my fingers. "So I guess this is the part where I ask, where did you learn to do that?"

"Through the Post Office. They pay the fees if you take classes on accident prevention and such. So every other year I sign up for First Aid."

"Have you ever brought anyone back to life before?"

"Shush," he says again, with that smile. He sits down next to me, hands draped across his knees. His socks don't match. Our shoulders touch.

"You know what I mean. I can't even spell resuscitate, much less do it."

"I brought Annie back once in class."

My adrenaline high is fading. I feel hollow all the way to my toes.

"You saved a life," I tell him.

"Well," he says, and stretches out his legs.

"Don't treat it like it's nothing. It's not nothing to her. Or to me."

"It's just what you do for someone," he says, and points to my hands. "Why do you need the phone?"

"I'm breaking up with Fernando," I tell him, and then I start to cry.

He reaches a long arm above our heads, pulls one of Mrs. Larsen's rumpled tissues off the counter, and hands it to me. When I look up at him, he's looking at me, and the space between us is a promise, a place I am willing to enter.

Somewhere in Omaha, Adam is driving his Civic while another woman puts her hand on the back of his neck. Somewhere is a woman, back against the wall, who would know what to say to this man with his crooked smile and tender, long-fingered hands. In Florence, Italy, the Neptune Fountain is filling up with wishes. And in this room, sitting against a Whirlpool fridge, is me, surfacing.

The Far Shore

MIREYA LOOKED DOWN at her legs in the middle of fifth-grade history class and discovered she'd turned into a fish.

Right in the middle of Mrs. Ho's lecture on Chinese history—or was it Korean history? No matter, since no one in class was paying attention to Mrs. Ho or Mireya.

She had in fact become a mermaid. Her knees had fused, her toes growing slender and long, webbed in fins. She pointed her chin straight ahead so as not to draw attention. Her upper body was the same old Mireya but now, below her waist, she had scales.

They were not hard or stiff as she would have imagined, like the armor of a knight or dragon; her scales were firm and flexible, like the clear plastic sheeting her father hung in the garage when he made repairs. They fit like a hard rubber glove or light chainmail, tight to her muscles. She squeezed her thighs and her hamstrings and felt the graceful curve of her flesh, fish-flesh, each fingernail scale iridescent as the wings of the dragonflies that came to rest on her mother's hibiscus, like the king salmon leaping up a fall of water on the nature shows she and Ben used to watch.

She wriggled in her seat. She couldn't wait to tell Ben she had grown a mermaid tail. She would say she slid out the window of her classroom and slithered to the gym and swam in the pool, swam and swam, and when she dove deep she found a tunnel she had never seen before, and she slid through a tunnel coruscating with light as though diamonds were embedded in the rock. Coruscating: Ben taught her that word when she helped him write his college application essay. It would remind him of their plan, their secret shared dream, that he would get into an Ivy League college and she would win the state spelling bee. He would be glad to hear her use one of his words.

She would spin a lengthy story for him, say she found the sea and tasted the warm salt and there were other fish and gulls sailing overhead like kites, and she lashed her tail and shed her clothes and dove in and out of water warm as a load of laundry, warm as a bedtime bath, and she would tell him she made a seaweed necklace and earrings of shells and there were dolphins—yes, there would be dolphins, because they were his favorite.

And she would tell the story so well that he would believe she had become a mermaid and open his eyes to see if it were true, finally he would open his eyes and smile at her, his eyes the same deep brown she remembered from long ago, the same Ben she had watched play basketball in the driveway, after dark, alone, the garage light shining like a moon on his face; he would come out of his long sleep finally and be Ben, the Ben she had known from before, the Ben she had known for always.

IN MIREYA'S HOUSE, there were lids for things. There were always proper containers: a breadbox for the bread, a flour jar for flour and a crock for sugar, a shaker for pepper and a shaker for salt. These things mattered. There were symmetrical pairs and sets of coordinated wash cloths and dish towels, matching sets of towels for the bath. For her mother, order meant serenity.

Ben's hospital room matched too but only in that everything was white: white light, white walls, white sheets for the bed. In Mireya's house they communicated by doors: open door meant enter, closed door meant studying, sleeping, shush. They tried to leave the door to Ben's hospital room open, inviting guests and visitors, but someone came and closed it in the night.

Without the light from the hallway only the dim light from the parking deck fell through his window. Mireya would wake in a sandwich of black, not knowing if she faced the floor or the ceiling, if her head pointed toward the window or the door. The darkness made the room enormous, its edges disappearing.

In the quiet the hiss of the oxygen machine by Ben's bed sounded like the breath of a dragon from one of her childish storybooks, a great red-winged dragon lying dark and brooding over his treasure, a watchful dragon that never slept. Mireya would reach out her hand slowly until she felt the bed and then she would feel across the bed until she found Ben's foot or ankle. She would keep her hand there, touching him, until she fell asleep again. If she were touching him she knew that her chair could not draw away from him in the moving vastness, that he would not accidentally float away.

"Mireya," Mrs. Ho said, "would you like to join us?"

The sea disappeared, sucked itself into a dry canyon. The dolphins bounded, blinked, and then vanished also. Quick as a flash the coral turned to dry scrub, the waving sea plants to tumbleweeds. Mireya squinted at Mrs. Ho. She heard the giggles around her as a folding curtain of sound, muffled underwater. Her eyes hurt from staring so long at the water, the sun's glare.

"Way to go, dopehead," came a low whisper from the back. "Mireya's a dopehead, just like her brother."

Her tail disappeared. She felt her legs, human legs, the skin dry and scaled like rock salt on a wintry road after the snow thawed. She curled her feet in her shoes and pressed each toe into the sole of her sneakers.

The voice was Jimmy Rosdale, and she would find him, during the afternoon recess, playing basketball, just as Ben used to do before he'd developed that tense look and started going out every night. She wanted so badly to make Ben smile again the way he smiled at her when she was a baby. Only their father could make him smile sometimes after dinner when he had his homework done, or on weekends when they disappeared into the garage. Mireya was no use to him after he learned she was no good at baseball.

"I'm listening, Mrs. Ho," Mireya said. "I find the Tang Dynasty—invigorating."

"Yes, scintillating," Mrs. Ho agreed dryly, and continued.

Scintillating, Mireya wrote in her book of words. It meant the same thing as coruscating. The school spelling bee would be held soon and as one of the older girls, practically a sixth-grader, Mireya had a chance. She wanted Ben to be proud of her. She didn't doubt that all those words and ideas he'd studied for his college prep class were still floating in his head somewhere, in a silent mist.

This land was an odd surface, Mireya thought. Why had that first fish ever tried to leave the water? And how was it he got a mate to follow? Mireya's textbooks wore the sticker: evolution warning. The Christians were worried that reading this philosophy of the scientists would endanger their faith.

But Mireya's Creator could handle dissenters. He slapped doubting Moses with a serpent and burning bush, back-handed Noah, the drunk. He dragged his chosen through the wilderness and drove Abraham to the top of a mountain with his son and a knife. Mireya read about it online, evolution with its magical connections, its tidy logic, in the half hour a night she was allowed to use the Internet. Her parents were not around to monitor Internet usage, but Mireya stuck to the rules. If she was bad, her parents anxious or unhappy, Ben would not want to come back.

There were so many things she didn't understand, though. How algae became a fish became a primate, all the gaps and leaps. It was just easier to trust that the terrible lord of her ancestors had created all things with a mighty breath, a holy and unutterable word.

"LOOK, IT'S DOPER Mireya." Jimmy Rosdale had the ball. He stopped and bounced it twice on the pavement when he saw her appear on the court. "What are you, stoned? Can't you see we're playing here?"

"My brother doesn't use drugs." Mireya looked at Jimmy Rosdale and no one else. He was shorter than the others; she was as tall as he was. His hair, as black as hers, stuck damply to his temples.

"Yeah, not so much now, I guess?" Jimmy jeered, while his teammates hooted encouragement.

"Get your girlfriend off the court, Roswell!"

Jimmy flushed. "She ain't my girlfriend." He didn't like the nickname, Roswell and its hint about aliens, since Jimmy's mother was Puerto Rican. She had cleaned houses before her marriage, so Mireya overheard at one of her mother's ladies meetings. One of her clients had been Jimmy Rosdale's father. There must be something shameful about being paid to clean other peoples' houses, Mireya gathered from their tone. Only goys didn't clean up after themselves?

Mireya observed Jimmy, looking for signs of slovenliness and neglect. His T-shirt had frayed sleeves and some of the letters of the team name were wearing off, but his hair was neatly trimmed. His mother's housekeeping ways must have thus far survived marriage to Jimmy's father.

Jimmy spat onto the asphalt between his shoes and Mireya's. "We don't have any dope for you, Traub. Go ask your brother."

"My brother," Mireya repeated, "is not a drug addict."

"Yes he is," Jimmy sneered. "Don't y'all remember this?" He addressed the faceless sixth-graders. Mireya didn't know any of their names; she focused on Jimmy's dark eyes. "Sure y'all remember that crackhead what drove himself and his buddies into that truck on the interstate this summer. Coming home from some party high as a kite, my dad said. Not two brains to rub together, the lot of them. They all shoulda been killed."

"He was not high!" Mireya screamed. "He wasn't even drunk!"

Her voice was swallowed by the tall forms around her. They waved like seaweed plants at the aquarium, growing up and up, lilting in the wet dimness with the lights that came from nowhere. In the silent wet Mireya saw their bodies cluster and move around from her, boys rounded like anemones, limber and healthy and whole. She saw rather than heard their mouths bubbling with laughter, saw her arm waft outward, saw her flat palm sink into Jimmy Rosdale's face and come away smeared with blood. A red arc spurted through the air as Jimmy's hands came up to meet his horrified eyes. He ran in the direction of the school and Mireya saw the basketball boys step back, parting like fronds, and she wiped her palm on her skirt.

On the TV cop shows that move could drop a man where he stood. She was disappointed that it had not dropped Jimmy Rosdale.

MIREYA SAT at the long gleaming dining table and thought about her knees. She pressed them together and waited for the fusion to happen. The house was quiet except for her grandmother, Nonna, putting away dinner dishes in the kitchen. Mireya lingered over her pudding and her self-made spelling dictionary. New words poured over her tongue like honey. She was learning them in clusters: Elevation. Apotheosis. Transcend.

One of the tall windows to the patio stood open and beyond it the insects tuned for their evening chorus. In the pool the neon glimmering water swished gently to one end and back. Beyond it the tailored garden fell into neat patterns of hedge and lawn tucked in at the corners, rooted with flowerpots and sloped with trees. It was her father's night to be at the hospital. Her mother had a meeting and would come home late. Nonna and Mireya would watch the news and then Mireya would practice her violin.

She was allowed to go to the hospital on Mondays, Wednesdays, and Sundays. Friday at dusk all three of them joined Ben to celebrate Shabbat, burning candles and saying the ritual prayers. Her mother sat before the heart monitor, the oxygen, all the other life-giving machines as if keeping guard over the outlet and its bristling cords.

There had been a discussion once—only once, angry and agonized—over the command against artificial life. Through it Mireya sat with held breath in her room, poised on her bed as though she thought it might collapse beneath her, pressing her fingernails into her palms. The red half-circles left their imprint for a long time, a line of coral scales.

Nonna was a much better cook than Mother. Mireya still remembered the boiled asparagus, too tough to chew, and her mother's rule that no one leave the table until they had eaten their vegetables. Their father, on call as always, swallowed his food whole and left to read medical literature in his study. Mireya sat at the cherrywood table, sulking, while Ben bit into a stalk and let it hang limply from his mouth.

He affected a nasal accent. "Do I have something in my teeth?"

Mireya giggled and did the same. "Do I have somefing—" The asparagus fell out of her mouth and she caught it, cold and sticky in her hand.

Ben dangled two green stalks from his ears. "Do I have something on my face?"

Mireya squealed and clenched her bladder muscles so she wouldn't pee from laughing. "Ben," their mother said as she stood at the china cabinet where she had been polishing her collection for an hour, trying to wait out her kids.

"What? I'm just asking. Mir will be honest with me." He put his hands down and Mireya saw him drop the stalks on the carpet behind his chair. The sight inspired her.

She threw a shoot from her plate at him. "Now you have somefing on your head!"

As punishment they were made to clean the dining room, kitchen, and then, the worst thing their mother could think of, the laundry room. Scrubbing the floor, Ben turned his sponge into a car and they raced, spewing bubbles. The floor was a swamp of dirty water before they were done.

Ben made everything interesting. When their mother told him to take her hand across the busy street he stuck his finger through her belt loop and towed her like a tugboat. As they waited for the school bus he made her guess how many fingers he held behind his back. She was never right, but it passed the time.

The best were the spring evenings when they played

catch. He wore his uniform in the front yard where all the girls in the neighborhood could see him and Mireya knew they could see her, too, with one of Ben's old gloves, her hair swinging as she threw the way he taught her.

She was the chosen one. She threw as hard as she could and kept inching forward though he yelled move back, move back, till her arm hurt and her gloved hand stung like bees, but she never told him this. Ben snapped the ball out of the air, threw himself on the ground as though touching first base, came up holding his closed glove like a trophy. He was announcer and crowd all in one.

"Home! Home!" Mireya would call, holding up her glove for one of his easy pitches, but he'd say, "No, you're tired, we're done," and casually look around to see whose eyes were on him. Mireya liked it best when none of the girls were dallying along the street and he would come into the house and check her homework and pretend to let her check his, shoving his indecipherable books at her and saying, "Hey, Mir, check my geometry proof, will ya?" and then they could watch TV.

THE DOCTOR SAID, when Mireya asked him, of course Ben could hear them when they talked. He could hear every word she said to him. It was like being in a very deep, long sleep, though his eyes were sometimes open. His brain had gone into a kind of loop and for the moment, for Ben, everything around him was like being underwater. He could hear and sense things, but it all felt far away.

NONNA STOOD IN the doorway to the kitchen, holding the phone in her hand. Mireya realized it had gotten dark.

"Your mom's meeting went late," she said.

"Mom's meetings always go late," Mireya said and mashed her fork into her pudding.

"She asked if you did your homework?"

"There was just algebra," Mireya said, dismantling the Tower of Babel she had made of her uneaten food. She separated the mighty edifice into separate ruins, the elbows of a five-pointed star. All of her algebraic equations had turned into waterlife: clumps of seaweed, curving starfish, sea horses with long eyelashes and coy spiraled tails. The borders of her math books waved with bubbles. Mireya liked them better that way.

"The principal wants to meet with your parents," Nonna said. "Were there problems at school today?"

She wavered in the doorway to the kitchen as though she were the housekeeper, the hired help. She wore her customary black sweater cardigan and a long dark skirt. A silver chain dangled from her eyeglasses, glinting against her silvered hair like erratic earrings.

"No," Mireya said. "No problems. But I saw a boy get hurt on the basketball court."

Nonna pulled a long thread from her sweater and stared at it. "Your principal seems to think there are problems with the boys in your class."

Mireya spooned a star point of pudding into her mouth and moved it over her back molars. "A ball hit him in the face. There was a lot of blood."

Nonna looked at the mezuzah in the doorway, looked at the parquet floor. Mireya knew she was praying for strength, for guidance.

"Mrs. Ho says that you have difficulty paying attention in class."

"Mrs. Ho," Mireya said, "has difficulty being relevant." She put the last of her pudding in her mouth and swallowed.

"They asked that I keep you home from school for the next two days." Nonna held the phone before her with both hands, like she would hold her siddur. Something she knew what to do with, unlike her difficult grandchildren.

"I can't possibly do that," Mireya said, scraping clean her plate. "Tomorrow is our class spelling bee, and Monday is the school-wide one. I am going to win."

Nonna looked at her as though she could see the traces of fish scales. Clearly she wished this was a problem Mireya's mother would handle. The mother who would be home late from an office meeting and too tired to deal with anything beyond taking off her nylons and pulling back the covers of her bed.

"Isn't it time you practiced your violin?" Nonna said.

Mireya brought her plate into the kitchen. "I will," she said. "As soon as I finish the dishes." She knew this was Nonna's least favorite job. She brushed her grandmother's hands as she reached to take the telephone. They felt dry and soft and nubbly, like rough wool.

"Who are you calling?" Nonna asked as Mireya ran water.

"The hospital," Mireya said. "I want to talk to Ben."

Nonna opened her mouth and no sound came out of it. Mireya thought suddenly that the whole kitchen might be underwater. The soft light from overhead fell in ripples, like a diffused light seen under the surface of the sea.

Ben understood, as she knew he would. He was glad she had defended him. When she described it to him, whispering over the phone so her father and Nonna could not overhear, she could tell Ben was imagining, with glee, the blood spurt that arced through the air after her hand encountered Jimmy Rosdale's face. She imagined that the Ben inside his head received the news with a cocky gleam to his oak-brown eyes and a quick sweep of his arm as if throwing an imaginary baseball, the way Ben swept off all news he didn't like. If Ben had not had the accident, if he had gone to the college their father picked out for him, everything would be different. She would not be able to talk to him like this.

MIREYA STILL didn't understand what the fights had been about, but they were always the same, and always bad. One night she curled up on his bed, against his leg as she always did, and he called her bug like he always did, but he read a comic instead of talking to her, and when she woke up later stiff and cramped she saw that in sleep he had pulled away from her and was sleeping on his side, one hand trailing on the floor, the lamp still burning.

Her mother saw her come out of his room and pressed her back as she guided Mireya to her own room and said, "You mustn't be sleeping in Ben's bed anymore, Mira, he's too old for that," and Mireya thought it funny that it was Ben, and not she, who should be too old for it; she was forever outgrowing things in those days. A year later he got his driver's license and stopped communicating with his family altogether, but Mireya marked that moment—of waking up under the glaring lamp, sleep gluing her eyes and her hair sweaty and Ben's body far away from her—as the moment she began to lose him.

MRS. HO WAS not pleased to see Mireya appear in class the next day. "I thought your grandmother said last evening that you didn't feel well," Mrs. Ho said, which Mireya understood as the lie that would have reached the ears of her parents.

She was tired of lying. "I feel very fit," Mireya said. "I feel exuberant."

At lunch Jimmy Rosdale leaned over her as she sat at the cafeteria table and dangled a forkful of limp and glossy green beans in front of her face. "No hanging around the court at recess, Traub," he said. "I've already had my vegetables today."

Inside her shoes Mireya felt her feet congealing. Her toes pressed together with sweat. It gave her the courage to look Jimmy Rosdale in the face. His eyes showed faint shadows of bruises. She had not quite broken his nose.

What would Ben do?

"You think my brother's a vegetable, Roswell?" she said. "That's what all your friends say about you."

Jimmy Rosdale turned the color of the roses that Mireya's mother grew in pots on their porch. The ringing bell signaled the end of lunch and the monitors came to the table, and Jimmy Rosdale could do nothing but glare before he walked away.

Mireya took a deep breath and walked to her classroom to study. Inside her shoes her toes stuck together, webbed and fortified.

She sat for the spelling bee with her knees interlocked, as though her calves were bound together with cord. Every word stood out in her head, carved in letters of fire. When they were down to three contestants she started silently reciting the Shema, the first prayer she had learned as a child. *And these words that I command you today shall be in your heart.*

Isabelle Hayes fumbled stationery and then it was two. They went back and forth for an hour, tireless, precise, and Mireya felt sweat running between her legs, gluing her ankles. The lights in her classroom burned hot and bright and relentless. Sophia Murphy went down on the word excision and with the next randomly generated word, recalcitrant, Mireya won.

"Mireya."

The sound came from far away, dangling in the air. In the soft currents of water surrounding her, the words were a quiet hum. Did fish sing to one another? Dolphins did. Mireya fanned her hands at her sides and the water moved around her, curving like a halo around her drifting head.

"Mireya!" A hand appeared in the dewy surface above her face, gripping her seaweed hair. Mireya sneezed water out of her nose as her mother yanked her head out of the bath.

"What are you doing?"

"Don't!" Mireya grabbed at the bath towel wrapped around her hips.

"Why are you—Mira, you know we have to get going . . . we're supposed to be at the hospital soon." She looked at Mireya's feet under the bathwater, wrapped in the towel like a mummy. The towel kept her heavy body anchored to the bottom. The last of the bath bubbles floated like a tiny raft over her former knees.

"I'm coming. I'll be ready in a minute." Mireya looked up at the face looking down at her. She could see where her mother's penciled-in eyebrows had become smudged. "Just a minute," she said again.

Her mother went to the medicine cabinet, opened the middle door. Mireya supposed she had not checked her cell phone messages yet.

"You can't watch me," Mireya said, pressing a hand to her thighs.

Mireya's mother did not have Mrs. Ho's smooth silken face or smooth-silk expressions. Her mother had a rake of deep lines across her forehead and small narrow lines running from nose to lips. One beautiful cluster of curls at her left temple never absorbed hair dye and remained a bright streak of silver, just like her own mother's hair. Mireya hoped she would have her own silver hair one day. It would look lovely in the sea light, shimmering under a setting sun.

"Fine. You have five minutes to dry off and get ready."

Mireya waited until the door was fully closed before she grasped the mummy wrap of her towel and began to unfold her fins.

"ECONOMY."

Mireya spelled the letters out on Ben's hand, squeezing each fingertip. Her spelling dictionary sat propped against Ben's leg.

He was in one of his sleeping periods, though sometimes when she squeezed his fingertips, she could get Ben to open his eyes. When he grimaced or smiled, what the doctor called involuntary responses, she knew he was responding to her. She raised their joined hands before his face and waved at him, but his eyes were closed, the lashes against his cheeks standing in points like the bristles of an anemone.

"Epitome," Mireya said aloud. "Epithalamus." She didn't even know what an epithalamus was, but she heard the doctors use the word.

Under the cheese slice of the half-open doorway stood three sets of shoes: her mother's brown heels, her father's polished black oxfords, the scuffed brown loafers of Ben's doctor. She wondered why they did not come into the room.

"Persistent vegetative state," the doctor said. Mireya caught a slip of the words, a scent floating past, intangible. "Chance of recovery . . ." His voice went into some depth beyond Mireya's hearing.

"Ethereal," Mireya spelled with a whisper, sliding each of her brother's fingers across her palms.

"Drug therapy?" her father said in a short burst of air.

". . . functionality greatly reduced." The doctor's words drifted slowly past. The click of padded shoes surfaced through the sussuration of their quiet voices. "Among the possible negative effects . . . "

Mireya's nose itched suddenly, sharply, as if she smelled fresh paint. She didn't want to release Ben's hand. She looked out the window at the leaves fringing the sky, flat as a pressed canvas. Her people had a prayer and a blessing for everything, and the words rolled in her mind like an ocean wave. *Blessed is this day and He who created it. How beautiful it is.*

"Exalted," Mireya spelled out on Ben's hand. Just like Anne Sullivan teaching Helen Keller in the book they had read at school. The word made the kaddish prayer came to mind, but she was afraid to recite it because it was also the mourning prayer and Ben might think it meant something. She would never give up on Ben.

"I've heard of cases of full recovery after a year," came her mother's crisp voice, like the principal calling the words of the spelling bee that would be held the next day.

"Excision." Mireya moved to the next word on her list. "Sophia Murphy screwed that up today. Can you believe that, Ben?"

"Severe damage," came the doctor's quiet words, a lap of sound in the long low mutter of their voices. " . . . disability . . . brain death."

An indrawn breath, then a high, thin tone she had never heard in her mother's voice. "End support? Malachi, you can't . . ."

The fringe of trees against the sky looked like a beaded skirt, like the hairs of an arm, like the thin floating fingers of seaweed. Any moment Mireya expected to see a fat otter go rolling through the sky, belly turned up to the heavens, to the stars hidden behind the blue. All this time she had thought her Creator above her and here He was in the white within-spaces she had to look so closely to see. *Extolled and honored, elevated and lauded be the name of the Holy One, blessed be He.* "E-x-t-o-l," she whispered, threading her fingers through Ben's.

She turned her eyes toward the window. It was not evolution but decay that made sense to her. That empty building across the parking lot, the old movie theater: eventually it would all return to the earth. The concrete wall would break apart, the glass would shiver and the steel corrode; the insulation would dissolve, the asphalt turn to powder and then dust, and how many years before this bizarre and symmetrical growth became a ruin, as ruined as Masada, as ruined as Temple Mount.

Someday it would matter simply because it was old, though now it stood empty because a better cinema had come along, a cinema with more screens, and brighter lights, and soft carpet, and nobody knew what to do with what was left sitting there, abandoned. Too much effort to restore or transform it, too much expense to tear down.

So much matter clumped together, so much energy compressed into a silent, still, abandoned space. And someday, after it became a ruin, someone else would wander through it and see what had existed: the cozy theater with its antique lights and painted walls, the velvet curtain before the cracked screen, the orchestra section, the wooden stage. To them, this ruined thing would be beautiful.

She'd been speaking aloud and hadn't realized it. She looked at Ben to find his eyes open. The doctor said he understood nothing, but Mireya knew. He'd heard outside the door. His eyes focused on her, trusting, lost.

"Persistent," she spelled out on Ben's hand. The doctor's loafers left. Her mother's shoes stood close to her father's, but Mireya heard no more voices.

"I'm going to win on Monday," she whispered to him. "I'm keeping up my end, okay?"

Night descended over the parking lot, a purple dusk shading its way to dark. Mireya watched the pine trees tossing their heads, sniffing the cooling breeze. *Blessed be the night, and He who created it. How beautiful it is.*

"It's all right, Ben," she told him. "I've got this."

Ben closed his eyes and the oxygen tube hissed. It sounded like the rhythm of waves. Her legs felt dry and her knees hurt and her cheeks felt odd, sticky. She draped her legs over the side of the armchair and put a hand on Ben's ankle to hold him.

Soon it would be complete. The last of the land Mireya would disappear and she would be transformed. She would have the body of a silvery fish and she would dive into that spirit sea, into that realm that had no limit. She would find Ben, wherever he was in that long dark tunnel he was trapped in, and she would pull him free to the open sea, to where the bottom fell away and there was only the ocean where the waves went on forever, scintillating, illuminated, coruscating with a thousand million points of light, and they would swim together into that place that was pure and perfect and whole.

ABOUT THE AUTHOR

Misty Urban is a fiction writer, medievalist, essayist, editor, and writing teacher. Her award-winning collections of short stories and assorted medieval scholarship explore the adventures of monstrous and misbehaving women, while her creative nonfiction explores the adventure of motherhood. In her historical fiction and romances, she likes to reward her ambitious, rule-breaking heroines with handsome heroes and happy futures. She holds an MFA in fiction and a Ph.D. in medieval literature and lives in eastern Iowa with a handsome park ranger, two small budding scholars, and a rather heavy collection of books. Find her online at mistyurban.net.

www.ingramcontent.com/pod-product-compliance
Lightning Source LLC
Chambersburg PA
CBHW071535120726

47907CB00014B/2171